Published by Joseph Naeem

Josephnaeem@aol.com

ISBN: 0989671100

ISBN-13: 9780989671101

Book Design by D. Williams

Text is set in Microsoft Word Calibri

12 Font

Daniela:

Enjoy.

D. Williams

Black Lives Matter!

The Killing of Mr. Floyd & Other Stories

By   D. Williams

Contents

II

IV

V

VI

VII

Acknowledgments

THIS BOOK IS A WORK OF FICTION: All characters are imagined. Any resemblance to actual persons living or dead or similarity to events past or present is mere coincidence. With utmost deference and honor this book is dedicated to Pearlie Mae Davis, aka Mama Tang. Just the thought of the strength and sacrifices of my mother, the daughter of former slaves with an 8th grade education is forever humbling. Having an absolute minimum of resources and support; day after day, year after year, Mama Tang habitually did the impossible as she raised seven children. Saying: "She did the best she could," minimizes Herculean feats of survival. Also, my love and respect to: Poppa, C.W., Dorothy, Geater, Lee Willie, Tootsie, JoAnne, Joseph, Davis, Barbara, and Barbara, Vera V., Inez: Also, DL, Top, Booker T. Dave Jr. Charles P., Aaron, Ben et.al.

Introduction:

The Killing of Mr. Floyd & Other Stories

Life isn't clarity, or sublime; it's just there, all the time, all the time, until it's not.

2006

First, we saw the green leaves falling, as we moved quickly past, and the thin trees jerking violently forward on impact;; then the thudding sounds before we heard the echoing gunshots. Three Black friends, together on a hot summer day in Southeastern Arkansas, who had hitched a ride to the lake, seven miles from town, for a swim. It was perfect weather for that last outing together before graduating high school.

Blazing afternoon sun filled a cloudless sky; a blue, blue lake; surrounded by red sandy loam soil, and cool clear water completed the ambiance. As usual, we didn't tell our parents about the trip to the lake because they would have told us not to go. It was the 60's during the Civil rights movement in the south; so they worried about things.

As we splashed in the shallows; avoiding two water moccasins gliding past in the small lake near the river, three White kids approached, carrying rifles. The taller of the two, cradling his weapon, said; "You nigras have to get out, we want to swim." Charles; the shortest, and thinnest of us three, weighing at most about a hundred pounds, standing 5'1 inches tall; pointing to the other side, shouted, "It's a big lake, you can swim over there!"

Gently, DL quietly mumbled, "Uh, Charles, they have guns, and we don't." The tall white kid responded, "Yall getting out and we're gonna swim right here!" Backing slowly out of the lake, picking up our clothes, as we moved to the trees; listening to Charles, "We should have kicked those motherfuckers asses!" he said as we walked quickly away.

If we had been hit and/ or killed by one of the stray bullets shot into the trees; our parents may never have known. It was not uncommon at the time, for those unheralded so called Civil Rights casualties; black children and adult males who suddenly went missing from local neighborhoods. Would they be called 'collateral damage' today?

Fortunately, childhood, youth, oftentimes comes with a mental and physical well being which guides and protects, through most trying and complicated situations; while enshrouding in a cocoon of normalcy. There are many names for that protection including; karma and luck, some even call it God.

Herein are stories of times long past and short presents; of places and people, nearly dead or dying. This country, America, as it grows and changes, reflects the lives of its people as does the following pages. Where to start: The beginning, with, the earliest memories of a 4 year old riding on the back of his mothers sack pulled through the fields; as she, wearing a black polka dot 'head rag', picked cotton near the river in a small southeastern Arkansas town.

Observations then and now are filtered through those memories of interactions with mother, grandfather; a former slave who told of his days down in the quarters on the old Week's Plantation; and six other siblings of that house at the end of the road called 'red pike' on mail Route #2 Box 581, Gould, Arkansas, leading out of town toward Douglas and 'the river'. Many of us live, seemingly, unaware of the connectivity to our earthly family; where the story of one of us is the story of all of us. These tales touch on aspects of all our lives and those varied similarities; and unique pieces of the puzzle that fit into the fabric of that colorful quilt of humanity.

D. Williams grew up in the south during the time of legal segregation of the races in the United States. He attended and graduated first in his class from Gould Colored High School. Four years in the United States Air Force; was followed by graduation from Pepperdine University in Southern California. He also completed teacher training at The University of Southern California and began a lifetime of teaching. That teaching experience, grades K-University was all in California where he thoroughly enjoyed the physical diversity of the state and its people. During those years of teaching he also found time to earn a Master's Degree from Sonoma State University, Juris Doctor from New College of CA, Law School and a PhD ABD from The University of California.

Now retired, he lives with his wife in a neighboring country.

The Wasp speaks of the earliest memories of a boy, in that small world of a very young child, living in a wood frame house; with a garden on the side, providing food for the family most of the year. The garden, the largest open area on the property, teeming with life, provided a sense of wild freedom for a small person. Here, no one told him what to do, how to do it; or where and how to be, along with all the other instructions that come with early childhood: Alone, he experienced curiosity, beauty, love, fear, a tinkling of race, and excruciating pain.

The Wasp

Arkansas morning, dew thick on the weeds, me and
a big horned snail outside, taking care of our needs.
Spring in the garden, the house beside; I was away
from the family; Mama Tang, Poppa, Joanne,
Tootsie, Lee Willie and Geater; still asleep inside.

A moment alone, a special, special thing, with the
blues and gold of morning, and what the sun
brings. Silver dew on old tomato plants, rotting in
gray, they're last year's remnants, now just in the
way. No crowding here, or unwanted sound, just
me, old plants, and this cold, cold ground.

Another step left, bare foot raised, squish on an old
potato, from pre-rot days. Quietly, moving
between the rows, and trying to keep the dewy
wetness, from 4 year old toes. Breathing the air of
that garden space, brought a chill to my chest, a
smile to my face.

It's nice to be outside, just God and me; to listen to
the quiet, as I flow through this norm, arms

wrapped around myself, trying to stay warm. One step across the other row, stalks reaching upward, where corn used to grow.

Was there purpose to my stride, direction to where I'd go? No just a child in a garden, within curiosity's glow.

Cool brown earth on bare feet, slight breeze touching my skin, damp brushes my leg, as deep silence, takes it all in. Seeing everything around me, feeling it too, warm and cool colors, emotions flowing through.

There, on a nest blending with plants winter dead; was one wasp, then two; four wasps in the morning dew. Reflecting sunrise on their heads, in the background of gray, the four wasps looked red. Possibly sensing dread, three flew away. The remaining wasp ignored me as I stared at its back, thinking, "Shall I continue to look, or do I attack?"

I needed a weapon; a hoe, rake or limb from a tree, but there was nothing near. Mind slowly working, concentrating on what I could see, looking down my body a plan came to me. Unzipping my pants; now knowing what I had to do; starting the deed, aiming for the wasp, as I peed.

Slowly, it rose into the air, and landed midway on my penis; I just stood there. When its tail rose, I thought, "What's it going to do?" As the tail slowly lowered, then I knew! Running crying into the house, finding Mama Tang; the wasp story, I started telling, while showing a penis quickly swelling.

We walked to Dr. Dixon's, the one Doctor in town, who treated all the same, white black or brown. Finally, we reached his office, penis painfully bumping my thighs, swollen from the wasp sting to triple its size. Examination over, moving slowly toward the door, I caught Mama Tang and the doctor's eyes; knowing I was the source of their humor, from their exchange of smiles.

Medicine: Is a memory of events when I was three or four years old. The experience was especially memorable because of its sensuality on so many levels, then, incomprehensible. Clarity and understanding came many years later as a young man, which added greater depth to my, understanding, and knowledge of my mother.

Medicine

Watching the tears flow, for an eternity; standing quietly observant, in that childhood awareness, adults and parents often fail to see. I must have been the baby, the only child home, the middle of a weekday morning, everyone else gone.

A baby, who thought adults didn't cry, they never got spanked so had no reason why. Besides, there was no one home to spank Mama Tang, so why would she cry? Seeing her scrubbing clothes in the washtub on the kitchen table, not understanding most of what she had to say, I just wished her tears away.

I heard the name Chris and "Why'd he have to die?" "Why did they kill him, why? why?" She was rubbing hard on the clothes, bent at the hip, a hand-rolled cigarette hanging from her lip. Tang, looking off into the distance, seemingly so tall; tears and talk flowing, as if I wasn't there at all.

   Afraid to interrupt, yet, I asked about the smoke, in the small room, now very thick, "Why does this smoke make me feel Sick?"Smiling through the tears Mama Tang said: "This smoke is medicine boy, for your mama's head."

Didn't make sense to me then; but I found that "Medicine "again; 15 years later; as I walked into a smoky room and asked; "What's that smell?" My naiveté was met with loud guffaws as I was told: "Reefer man, weed, you know ganja, marijuana!"

Hunger Is: What does it mean to be hungry? Is the experience only partial; incomplete, without the applicable words, thought, knowledge or description?

Without those words, thought, knowledge or description; hunger is physical, and is felt. One who'd always had that feeling; how would they know that that physical pain was not a normal part of life and living? What is hunger?

Hunger Is

Having to go to school with no breakfast, and get the best grades in your class with no lunch; and to do your homework with no dinner: Hunger Is:

Having to go to school a second day with no breakfast; get the best grades in class for a second day with no lunch; and to do your homework with no dinner: Hunger Is:

Thinking four days of school without food was normal: Hunger is: Having a constant headache and stomach pain, from your earliest memory, until your first complete meal at age 18 as a young military recruit: Hunger Is:

Shockingly, being told for the first time in my life, at age 18; that I would get in trouble if I didn't eat all the food I put on my plate!

Hunger is...

Mr. Sip much like older adults I knew, rarely spoke. Every time I saw him, he wore the same clothes: Clean, but looking the same. I never saw him angry, but I did see Mr. Sip smile: Never saw him have a conversation with anyone; adult or child. He'd say "How Do" to adults and children who spoke to him, otherwise Mr. Sip walked silently past.

Mr. Sip

"Eyyyyyyyyyyyyyyyyyyyyyyyyyyyyyyyyyyyyyyyyyyyyyyyyy yyyyyyyyyyyyyyyyyyyyyyyyyyyyyyyyyyyyyyy" I think that was the sound. Loud and long we all could hear across the tracks, in the 'Colored' part of town. Each day we'd hear it, many a time. He must have been napping and dreaming, wonder what was on his mind? No one actually saw him when he yelled,

"Eyyyyyyyyyyyyyyyyyyyyyyyyyyyyyyyyyyyyyyyyyyyyyyyyy yyyyyyyyyyyyyyyyyyyyyyyyyyyyyyyyyyyyyyy But it became commonplace, day after day; we could hear it blocks away. Loud at the beginning, fading low to silent at the end, lasting a few seconds, then starting again. I don't remember the first time I heard it, nor the last; now, just fading bits of childhood's past.

We became friends, me and Mr. Sip. I'd stop and visit on the day, when allowed to go to Cousin Lela Mae's. His house was along the way; one long room; cooking/heating stove at the far end; pipe up and out of the ceilingless roof, metallic circle of gray tin.

Black man; Blue overalls, all he ever wore, Brogan shoes, walking Saturdays to the store. I liked stopping at his house because he shared what he had, biscuits and sorghum syrup, for a child with nothing, that wasn't bad.

Front door opened when I knocked, he'd get a plate; two biscuits and molasses, then watch while I ate. I don't remember when I stopped stopping, it saddens me today. Did I even say goodbye to Mr. Sip, or just outgrow him and fade away?

Is that how it's always done? One day a thoughtless departure, from the ones who taught us to love, to give, expecting nothing in return. They are those who taught us to stand, to walk tall, to show others how to learn. Belatedly, I thank you Mr. Sip, for helping a little boy grow, and for being a better neighbor than you will ever know.

81 Junction is very special for many reasons. Even today when I visit home, the drive takes me past 81 Junction. During my last visit in 2011, for the first time; that fabled corner looked barren and empty. Nothing was standing on that special side of the roadway. With heavy heart, I noticed that the building I'd looked for on that special corner, on all my more than 40 years of trips home; the building that housed the 'Jook Joint" in this story **81 Junction**: Like my mother Tang, was gone.

81 Junction

This was a time when I was too young for school and too young to drive. We didn't own a car but four or five times a year we traveled from Gould to Woodson, Arkansas to visit Aunt Alice. On the trip home we'd make one stop.

I remember the stinging, the burning in the eye: As the pain increased I kept thinking, "Don't be a baby; don't cry. Don't cry."Staring amongst the sea of legs, I looked for Mama Tang. Through the haze, finally I saw her, slow dancing. The music made my ears ring. A blues playing guitar man was yelling, "Ain't it the troof!"Through the undulating smoke, I saw the sparkle of his one gold tooth.

There was urine smelling whiskey, vinegar smelling wine, tight dressed ladies all looking fine. Tang in her youth: Shapely figure, face sublime, a small glimpse of joy, before ravaging poverty and time. She was smiling, and dancing happily, saying hello to everyone as she moved past me.

A four year old kid, quietly unseen, curiously ingested a very adult scene. Varied colored clothes and Negro people abound; feeling the close camaraderie, part of the surround. Puffy Camel nimbus clouds and strata Pall Malls; made the one light dangling from a frayed wire like a sun; with a nose burning smell.

81 Junction was the name of the place, where US Highways 65 and 81, met face-to-face. There, on that corner, between Woodson and Gould, I learned my very first lessons, at Jook-Joint school. Yes, I was too young to be there, and too short to see, over those physically taller, and wiser than me.

Through the forest of legs; I saw the many faces so free, in each other's arms smiling with glee. Tang and the adults, the smoke in my eye, a memory I'll treasure till the day I die. As the years slipped past with various trips to and fro, on my returns home, I'd always check, to see if the building was still there? I had to know.

Over the years as I did school, basketball and girls, including the military and the California college world; out of the corner of my eye, returning home that building I'd see; and those memories; those memories; would overwhelm me. The gravel parking lot, the crowd, and idiosyncratic music of that place and time, disappearing without mention, from fading survivor's minds.

I still feel the burning smoke, and smell the stale wine, hear the mournful guitar, and the joy of that time. The memory is most clear, one of its kind. It's so special, because it's just Mama Tang's and mine. What I saw that night I'll never again see, Mama Tang brightly smiling and so very happy.

The Chicken: Is a story about my grandfather, who we called 'Poppa'. He often surprised me because he was so different. He inadvertently, taught me the word illiterate, shockingly; once I saw him sign his name with an elaborate "X". A former slave, Poppa was very wise, and a uniquely, interesting person. As a matter of fact, to this day; Poppa was the wisest man I've ever known. Here, in this story he needed both; wisdom and a steady hand. Although, the steady hand he did not have.

The Chicken

Thick beige dust on a day so hot, Southeast Arkansas summer on a backyard lot; five foot wire fence chickens surround, hard packed earth below the dusty ground. Mama Tang said, "Bring me that old gray hen, she ain't layin no mo, make a nice stew in an hour or so."

We kids were happy to oblige, chasing circles and across the yard from side to side. Lee Willie was the oldest, around seven or eight, the rest of us following with a younger gait. Running and laughing, having a great old time, as the chicken easily avoided us without really trying.

Back and forth, noisily across the yard, again and again, we chased the chicken past the smokehouse and the potato bin. We couldn't wait to see what happened when we brought her In. Tang would grab it by the neck and swing the weighted body around, until the head twisted off and the chicken hit the ground.

Being insensitive twisted kids, this was where our fun began; running from the headless body, jumping up and down, the neck squirting blood, again and again. We couldn't catch the chicken, though we really did try. It must have known that it was meant to die. Barefoot laughing children, running bird, a surreal scene, untouched by life's sadness and all future mean.

Cutting sharply through the dust and the swirl of the day, we heard Poppa's voice say, "You chillun get out of the way!" By now Tang was yelling too, "Run, ya'll better run, Poppa's coming out there with his gun."Gleefully, we complied. Diving behind chicken coops and the woodpile, here was major drama, and so much fun.

Peering from hiding, seeing Poppa, push open the screen and stand, in the kitchen doorway; his 38 in his hand: I remembered his palsy, and how he shook when I brought his morning cup. Daily, spilling coffee into the saucer and shakily sipping it up.

I'd look on in wonder as the saucer banged against his teeth, making a clacking sound. So, I asked, "Since when, could Poppa, with his palsied hands, shoot a running hen?" Now all was quiet in the yard, chicken strutting boldly toward the right fence; we, staring from our safe places waited in suspense.

Poppa's hands, wobbled left and wobbled right, keeping the walking chicken clearly in his sight. The explosion caught us by surprise, hunkered down near the earth, closed eyed. We opened to a headless chicken, bouncing across the yard. Poppa did in an instant, what we'd found impossibly hard.

On that still blue cloudless day, the large puff of gun smoke, floated slowly across the gravel road. One shot, that's all it took. It happened so fast, no time to look. Red fire from the gun barrel, gray smoke so very thick; Poppa was old and shaky, but also quick. The chicken, one minute walking possessed of its head; then a bleeding jumping neck though already dead.

Acrid smell of gunpowder, ringing in the ears, made another Poppa story, from childhood years. Watching his crooked back as he moved away, we listened to the neighbors and the words they had to say. Mr. Buddy Murray: "I heard only one shot that chicken can't be dead. Did it get away?"

No longer did he insist, when he saw Mama Tang, the dusty, headless evidence in her fist. The neighborhood kids came running; they too had heard the boom; and saw the smoke blowing across the street. They were pushing into the backyard, lo oking much like us, in hand-me-down clothes; dusty bare feet.

One look at the chicken head; the blood on the ground; they started talking about the shot, the fumes, and the loud, loud, sound. All peering at Poppa again; his smoking gun; palsy hand.

Stepping around the corner of the house, was Mr. Alec, wearing his usual one brown shoe and an unmatched boot: saying, "He might have the shakes, but damm, that old man can

shoot!"

Mucie: Tells of my confrontation with a female friend in the neighborhood when I was 6 or 7 years old. She was ten at the time; taller and faster than I. When my older brother Lee Willie and his friend Ike; who wouldn't open the gate for me, tell this story, they claim that I was 18 years old at the time and that Mucie was a tiny 12 year old girl.

Mucie

She was a little older and taller than me, braided hair and pleasant to see. We were outside playing at her house as we often did, some silly game with a ball, just being kids. Older and bigger Mucie often let me know, that her way of doing things was the main show.

She wanted the ball and so did I, so I snatched it and hit her, but she didn't cry. Thinking, "What now Mr. Suicide shall I run?" In races with the boys Mucie always won. Seven year old legs churning thinking; "I gotta win today!" Mucie close on my tail, and my front gate; was still a block away.

Flying over the rocks and gravel, I was running hard, getting away, knowing, "Half a block I'll be in my house, safe today." Just seconds ahead of Mucie, I yelled to my older brother Lee Willie, standing in our front yard; "Take the chain off the gate!"

He looked at his friend Ike, and shook his head, "No." as both smiled at Mucie, my onrushing fate. As I Grabbed the gate chain, trying to get in, Mucie relentlessly; rained blows on my head and back; again and again and again.

When she tired of pounding me and finally walked away, Lee Willie and Ike, smirks on their faces, took the chain off the gate, with nothing to say. Through humiliatingly snotty sniffles, I said to my brother, "I'm telling Mama Tang you wouldn't help me.

Seething with anger, I dashed in the front door, told Tang the story, and got whipped some more. "Boy, you let a girl do that to you? If Lee Willie had helped I'd whip his ass too." Later, alone on the back step, pondering the events of the day, my laughing brother and his friend walked past; going to Ike's house to play.

The Killing of Mr. Floyd: is a story about my mother's boyfriend; who seemed to have been around forever, though arrogant, selfish, mean and cruel, especially to my mom. Mr. Floyd, was one of those Black men of the south who bought into the system that judged folk by the color of their skin. As a 'light skinned' Black man he couldn't help but show his assumed superiority to my dark skinned mother and her kids. Mama Tang obviously loved that mean and cruel man. Our grandfather did not.

The Killing of Mr. Floyd

The cotton field over our back fence ran as far as the eye could see. At its very center, barely visible, stood a lone house and a very large oak; rumor said it was once a hanging tree. We stood behind the wire fence in the yard watching the start of 'The Walk', Tang and Floyd together, holding hands like lovers; her with a big smile, looking forward to a happy mile.

Knowing how it always ends, we thought, "God, not that walk again." Tang on the return, head down, face bad, and tears flowing into the yard, so, so sad. Four sets of kid's eyes, staring hard at Floyd, who ignored us in his guilt, seemingly annoyed.

What should we do? Lee Willie, Tootsie, Joanne and I certainly didn't know. Just little kids wishing we'd hurry up and grow. Time and time again, as they started their walk, I wanted to yell, "Why do you continue to go?" Big smile on her face, by now she should know. The minute they're out of town, Floyd's real reason would show!

Out where no eyes could see him make the bruises, as he beat her down. Why can't Mama Tang see past the phony smile, and remember that he'll hit her, before the 1st quarter mile. Day after day, why must he hurt, hit and be so mean? Is Floyd in love too: or is that something only women must do?

Love, maybe children three through nine couldn't understand, but we could hear the thud of a fist and the cuff of a hand. Thinking: "Someday I'll be bigger, bigger than he, then I'll 'double dog dare' that monster to hit me!"We'll see. We'll see.

Certain things just weren't meant to be. I never got a chance to carry out my plan. Tang took care of that unhappy, abusive man.

The slap sounded loudly on that clear blue day, four kids like statues suddenly frozen in play. Lee Willie took the lead; Joanne, Tootsie and I to follow; quickly through the front door to the couch in the kitchen, now too scared to swallow.

Floyd's light skinned offending hand; rested quietly on the knee, of his 6'5 inch frame, much, much, taller than me. That white looking Black man with his wavy 'good hair' did the unthinkable again, and now was just sitting there.

Tang was crying softly, hand covering his crime, repeating a scene witnessed by her children, many a time. Why does she stay with a man who hits and makes her cry? Reckon we were too young to know and understand why. Seven years old, I wasn't the youngest child, JoAnne had that honor, and she was only five.

Tootsie was six and Lee Willie had just turned nine. On our sagging brown couch sat that wicked man, smiling at the tears on our faces, the trembling anger in our stands. Fists balled so tightly they hurt our little hands; Lee Willie gives the word we'd take that old man.

Looking up between sniffles, Tang said, "You chillum, get out of here!" Eyes dripping, trying to hold back the tear, we started backing away, watching Floyd's sneer. Thinking: "Today you're big and tall, but remember, we won't always be so small."

Days and weeks passed, walking home from school, near Miss. Francis' corner house with tall pecan trees that kept it shady and cool. A large adult crowd was in our front yard, easily seen from there; curiosity; the feeling overwhelmed my fear.

Moving across the yard through the tall legs; I was able to see at a level, just above the knee. Unspoken words, loudly said, I could only hear them when I'd see a nodding head.

Into and through the living room and the kitchen door; where lay Floyd on his back, dead on our kitchen floor. Leaning close enough to touch; I looked closely at the hole, center forehead and the protruding gray matter outlined with a small circle of black blood.

Here, nothing was said to children in the silent surround, as I pushed through the crowd, moving people around, to be close and certain that Floyd was down. The story was there, easy to see, how those events came to be. Our twisted back door, hanging by one hinge; Floyd's big foot must have kicked it in.

There were two bullet holes above the door, another in the ceiling and one in the floor. The bullet in Floyd's forehead brought the count to four. Backing from the kitchen, past Floyd again, I noticed blood on his shirt, where another bullet went in. Mama Tang couldn't shoot straight, unfamiliar with a gun, but on this day, she got the job done.

A lone white man now moved through the crowd, murmurs in the silence, became suddenly loud. Four kids on the front steps, watching that day; at Tang looking back from the police car, slowly driving away. Home that night, scared and alone Tang shot Floyd, and now she too was gone.

No school the next day, Tang was away. The silence was still deep in that house with no sleep. Huddling together, nobody cried, but we stayed away from the kitchen where Floyd died. Dragging past morning, to early afternoon, when Tang came home, ending the gloom.

Joyful kids, no more fear, it's gonna be alright now that Tang's here. Looking a little frazzled from her night away, we sat with the neighbors listening to her say; she'd had dinner in a jail cell with an unlocked door, an overnight stay and not one day more.

Yep, that's how the story ends one man's words sent her home again. No charges, no trial, no prosecution, no legal pronouncements from a justice tome. Calling Mama Tang by her first name, the young policeman said,

"Pearlie, go home."

The Coming: Do you remember the first time you saw a person with skin color different from your own? This is a story about a totally unexpected experience in a place where sameness and repetition were the norm. For the very first time in the history of that small Southern segregated Black/ White town, the community was exposed to an unexplored difference. The children had heard bits and pieces regarding such differences in their school classrooms; but there were no pictures in the textbooks. The public library may have provided pictures but it was for whites only.

The Coming

Summer Saturday Morning in the tiny Arkansas town, where 'Red Pike' was the main road, heading west, to the river's black bottomland farms; which on this day, added a heretofore, unseen diversity, to our Black/White norms.

Open pickup trucks rolled past one after the other; workers on the back, lining both sides; drawing ever nearer, to the end of very long rides. We'd picked and chopped cotton in those very same fields out the river way, but not today.

Today, Black faces lined the road called 'Red Pike'; all ages, grandparents, parents; my aunt and her baby, the youngest kid. And other children and toddlers; peering behind adult pant legs thinking they were hid.

The spectacle of spectacles that we were all out to see, the very first in the lives of us in that town: The folk riding the backs of those trucks weren't

Black or White, "My God," they were Mexican, they were Brown!

Hallway: Is about a child aging up and becoming the oldest male, 16, in the household and a slightly paranoid parent.

Hallway

A child with older siblings may remember; though you love them; the lifelong dream of waiting for the oldest to age up, and go away. If there are three ahead of you, two are O.K; but the third, the one closest to you is always in the way. Gotta be the boss, over and over again, because he is older and bigger, avoid his path, no way to win.

But, he also had to do the scary things when he became number one. Answer the door when a stranger knocked, while Mama Tang held the gun. Lee Willie, while doing that and the other thankless jobs that comes to the oldest child, would sometimes mumble and make a quiet fuss, while we younger kids, looked at each other; and smiled, glad it wasn't us.

There was one other major responsibility, of which we never knew, because we were always sleeping, when Lee Willie had it to do. Those other responsibilities, to soon I was able to see, because suddenly, the oldest child was me. Now, Mama Tang awakened me to walk the floor, because of noises only she heard, in our kitchen or at the back door.

Together we'd creep down the hallway, Tang; pistol in hand leading, followed by me, now the oldest child; helping, feed the fear of her need. On that night, Tang forgot she woke me up, walking closely behind, in the unlighted hallway: This week for the 2nd time.

Turning suddenly, she pressed the 38 to my forehead. In the pre death silence, I whispered, "Tang, it's me." Snatching the gun away, she angrily asked; "Why you walking behind me boy! What the hell's wrong with you?"

"Because you told me to."

Watch Meeting: Growing up in the South; I came to know Watch Meetings: Held in churches and/or homes for hours or days with children on the outer fringes of the Watch. I participated in one.

Watch Meeting

I was poppa's favorite, or so, as adults, my brothers and sister told me. Thinking back and listening to their explanations of how they knew: I think that that may have been true.

Molasses slow morning; heavy hints of dread: Poppa in all the years was always the first out of bed. Not today. Poppa, my advocate; often found reason to encourage me in school; bragging to the neighbors: "That Donnie, he ain't nobody's fool!"

Later, I walked into the living room where Poppa now sat with Mama Tang and Miss Mildred; a neighbor from across the street: Odd, because Poppa rarely sat with others; especially outsiders.

Focused concentration; mentally and physically trying to see; saying nothing, looking hard at Poppa as his unblinking eyes looked back at me. A sound in her voice with a hint of doom: "Poppa is a little sick." Mama Tang said as she left the room.

In my 16 years; Poppa had never been sick, never even seen a doctor. This couldn't be; I looked again at Poppa; lowering his eyes and showing what I didn't want to see. Eyes about the room as my intensity grew; three bowed heads; then I knew.

Returning from the doctor, with nothing to discuss:
To begin the watchful waiting, a silent serenity of
unstoppable ends; as it enveloped us. Moving
slowly with expression; "I'm going to bed." Only I
looked at him; witnessing the gravity; the lonely,
poignant simplicity; the finality, of what Poppa
said.

More hours, we three sat in the front room,
watching late into the night; for the inevitable.
Finally Mama Tang said: "Go check on Poppa." All,
knowing before I stood; what I was going to see:
Slowly moving toward Poppa's door, fear walked
with me.

Without a knock, into his cold, cold room; I looked
at the familiar pictures still on the walls, pipes on
the stand; and Poppa's favorite chair at his desk.
Lastly, standing beside his bed, I looked down at
Poppa; ashen faced, stiff toed, on his back; open
mouthed, with open unseeing, fright filled eyes of
pain and death.

The Greyhound Bus: This is a story about a trip I took to my childhood home in Arkansas a few years ago. Here, I a Vietnam Veteran saw for the first time; death and a love of killing in a man's eyes as he looked at me. However, that may be the least important part of the story.

The Greyhound Bus

Greyhound Bus Station, Pine Bluff, Arkansas; one hour stop in the middle of the night. Passengers shuffled in, Colored to the left and White to the right. Standing on the dividing line to enforce segregation, stood a Black cop, death in his eyes, hand on his gun. The year was 1984 but those folk didn't seem to know, or care, that 'separate but equal' supposedly ended back in 1954.

Here, the rules of the Old South remain, your life, if you refuse to play the game. Maybe my California clothes were the reason why I became the focus of the cop with death in his eyes. I didn't travel from California to Arkansas to die and certainly wouldn't be the fool to challenge his rule. Doesn't matter what the Washington Courts say, the racists in Arkansas still have their way.

The waiting rooms' Colored sign hung in the same spot; though painted over, folk's places, all knowing; even if only the "ed" was showing. The White sign is probably painted over too; but these folk do what they do. The cop only has the authority to arrest or kill Blacks; so White passengers may sit where they like.

But even the Whites from California and the North, who were talking to Blacks before coming inside, knew how to act and where to go. They sat formally on the White side; head up oblivion, like they belonged there. Blacks on the Colored side knew the rules too; head down, no eye contact with anyone, especially Whites and the cop from the neighborhood they knew.

I sat quietly taking in, the leftover information, from that to slowly fading historical blend. The three bathrooms remain, Men, Women and Colored, the signs painted over but used the same. It's been said that eyes are windows we use to look out, but windows are two way and also allow others to look in.

Discreetly peering into the open eye windows on both Colored and White sides of the room, I was again reminded of why I left the South: the danger, and persistent feelings of impending doom. Racism in California and the North is most often subtle and indirect; though just as real: But racism in the South is more active and will still kill.

II

See: Moving outside ourselves and the books we read, the songs we listen to and the conclusions we draw from the solitude of our own psyche, one encounters others. Sometimes, no matter how hard we try, it is difficult to impossible, to establish relationships with folk whose views and life experiences are very different from our own.

See

Hands on the pen again, not sure I want to see,
what comes out the end, of today's reality.

You see brick, I see stone, you see body, I see

bone.

You see a bird, I see a feather. You see blue sky, I
see the

weather.

You see love, I see need. You see the roses, I see

weed.

Beautiful dresses; long, long trains, I see down
pillows and longer

chains.

You see round, I see square. You see here, I'm
really over

there.

You see time, I see light. You see fear, I see a

fight.

You see friend, I see trend. You see beginning, I see

pretend.

You see comedian, I see a clown. You see a Rolls
Royce; I see a Honda stripped down.

You've been over there, been her too. It means
nothing to me, but everything to

you.

Gimme Some There are times when we feel that we are standing glued to one spot while kaleidoscopic life events whiz past at the speed of light. We want to be a part of all of it, jump in, but shyness, fear, trepidation or other insecurities hold us back from this essence of earthly experience.

Gimme Some

Life's regenerative juices, they run, run, run. Folks all yelling gimme some; gimme some.

Burning ever brightly, searing all slightly, but not enough to say, keep it away. Yes, there are drawbacks, misfortune and doubt, it's a burning flame, but don't put it out!

While serving down here, we do the best we can, trying to live good lives, as God's woman and man: Respecting all creatures, microscopic and small, knowing the creator, meant life for us all.

Live in harmony; multivariate surroundings, colored experiences, rejoicing, resounding. Sounds of being, passed from you, passed to me, and to all others, throughout eternity.

Feel the sadness, hear the pain, touch the hope, and embrace the gain. Yes its life, can't you see, flowing so quickly, right past me. Stop the hours, quiet the drum. We all need time to get some.

Big Fat Rattlesnakes This story is about a recurring dream I used to have about rattlesnakes. When I lived in Sonoma County, daily, I ran in a state park near my home where rattlesnakes on the trail were common. Once I even threw my keys at one blocking the trail. The snake did not move.

Big Fat Rattlesnakes

Big fat rattlesnakes, along the running trail, thick as my upper arm, from head to tail: Same old dream, fresh new fear, I know it's not real, but when dreaming, it's true here. Hundreds coil and slither, as I move up the hill: Circling front and back, covering all sides; rattling scales and tails, no place to hide.

Dare I retrace my steps at a quick pace? Can I get through them all? Will I win this race? 'Here goes nothing' as I reversed my run, moving fast like a bullet from a downhill gun.

Past one snake, past two and three, counter to the path, they're moving away from me. Eyes darting here and there, I see as many as I can. If I miss just one, it could mean the end.

Gaze panned slowly, to the right side, a dark brown head, caught me in stride. Stretched full length, it hooked my running pants. Sharp, sharp fangs, snagged the cloth: Could it strike again, before I got it off?

Starting to slip and slide on the loose rock, with
three pounds of snake banging against my sock:
Beginning to pray, hoping it was some kind of test,
God being the only way to get out of that mess.

Awakening thanking him for intervention so timely,
alive free and snake less; mercy me! Mercy me!

Shaking Red is from a time when I commuted 3 hours a day to work in 'The City' (San Francisco). On this day, at the end of another long commute week, I was unprepared for the additional drama; noted in the following story. Also, Po-Po is slang for Police.

Shaking Red

His shirttail was hanging, with an open collar, below a gray stubble mahogany face; new wave afro hair, all out of place. Red car shaking, as he pulled up to the door, the brother left it running as we entered the store.

I moved to the front counter as he went to the back. A 6'4 inch coffee colored sister, a bit thick and wide, was suddenly standing next to me, on my right side: Eyes only for the brother somewhere in the back, expectant, encouraging him to initiate some act.

Watching the budding drama from my one good eye I only wanted gas and a silent goodbye. Big sista spoke to the Indian clerk, still looking to the rear of the store.

Missing her words, in another space; thinking: "An empty gas tank brought me to this tension filled place." From the eyes of the Sikh clerk, I began to see, expectancy, fear, resolve and suspicion; directed at the back brother, after bouncing off me.

Collecting my change, I eased toward the door, six eyes of doom; staring at the back of the room. I'm out, thinking, "What a weird 7-11 store; certainly won't stop here anymore."

Leaning on my bumper, pumping the gas; freeway automobiles whizzing quickly past: The shaking red car, was suddenly beside my pump: I could feel the brother's eyes as his car shook and jumped.

The end of a long work week and a longer commute; I thought," What the hell could he be trying to see?" The long pause ended as shaking red pulled away. Guess he decided my interruption was inadvertent, or when the Po-Po's come, I'd be gone, or have nothing to say.

Shaking red's taillights dimly faded up the hill, as in rolled the Po-Po's black, quiet and still. Much more going on here than selling snacks and gas: What had I stumbled into like a dumb S?

My tank was full and I got out of that lot, thankful for God's protection in another situation hot. Rolling home I remembered, my friend Tommy Lee, killed, walking into a gas station robbery.

Whatever Happened: Is about memory and memories which most of us have forgotten. A quote from the French Historian Pierre Nora seems fitting: "We speak so much of memory because there is so little of it left."

Whatever Happened

Whatever happened to a time not so very long ago,
to the people that was us, the ones we used to
know? Whatever happened to that place, safe for
all to come and go?

Whatever happened to neighbors? Do they exist
anymore? Remember them; they were special
friends, more than just the people next door.

Whatever happened to the land of the free that
locks down generations of color, to protect us from
me? Whatever happened to the country, I grew up
in, that Lassie safe world of Rin-Tin-Tin?

Whatever happened to caring, for ones fellow
man? How did we twist it, to use and abuse
quickly, and use again?

What about help for all, struggling to live well?
From whence came the change to, "Forget them, I
want mine, they can all go to hell!" Whatever
happened to the 'Golden Rule', when to do unto
others didn't make one a fool?

When did we become the society that we are, so
mean-spirited and cruel, after traveling so far? It

matters not how cold, many of us have become, we can still change the model, one, by one, by one...

Corners: too is about life and day to day living; about our attitudes toward constantly impacting cataclysmic; commonplace and definitive events. "It's not always circles; there are also squares!"

Corners

They come at the speed of light, with changes, changes, blurring sight. Corners are square and sharp on the edges, quick to cut and bruise unwary pledges.

Everything settled, led to think all was fine, when out of nowhere: Something hits you blind. Where did that come from? How could one know, that around that corner they should not go.

A corner, just a corner, angles always the same; right turn pain, left it remains. Should you retreat and avoid the attack, of course no. It's just a corner, turn and go: Corners crowd, cloud, and attempt to shroud, as they scream; very, very loud.

They embarrass, they harass, will knock a brother flat on his ass.

Corners, corners, are coming my way, why can't I move, and avoid them, for just one day? Thankful for the hand, that snatched me around, to stand mutely watching corners; corners crashing down.

Thick: Obesity has been identified as a major epidemic in the USA, especially in the Latino and Black communities. Consequently, we see a surplus of women and men with a "Few extra pounds..." out there looking for a hook-up with a brother or sister. Or, worse than that; after the hook-up, both start out as a thin couple and then one may become singularly 'thick'.

Thick

Obesity, ethnicity, expanding sizes, triple XXX's fantasizing. The fat is going around; especially to sistahs; Black and Brown. Much wider hips, bigger around, protruding tummies, crack showing frowns.

Totally unaware of how BIG they are, most still thinking, "I'm just a slightly buxom ethnic star." Don't dare mention size, or those triple X clothes, you get all kinds of attitude and a turned up nose.

Words to avoid staying in her good graces: obese, fat, diet, salad, cholesterol or workout places. Big boned, healthy, and stout are OK: euphemistic lies that never get in the way.

So, when your honey gets 'thick', what can you say? "Stop this feeding frenzy, starting today!" What if she was 'stout' from the very beginning? Is a few added pounds good reason for ending?

Maybe she was just pleasantly 'plump', with a hip hugging figure and a very cute rump. Now,

everything has grown, changing the love you'd
known. All soooo much bigger; go figure.

Mention Weight Watchers, she doesn't want to
hear it; prepare the right foods, she won't come
near it. She wanted it her way, I left that day.

Now I'm doing much better than I've ever been,
because my new main squeeze is so, so thin. When
the triple X sistahs see us, their faces do frown;
because my new thin love ain't Black or Brown.

Sistahs may look with their jaws all tight, but I can
get my arms around this woman at night.

Prey: Speaks to a society uncomfortable if a Black or Latino male is not in Jail, prison; on probation or parole. Find pictures of Latino and Black males; posted in police ready rooms, in towns and cities all over the country. Men of color who have committed nor been charged with a crime. In a police state police 'suspicion' or to dare question ("argumentation") is equivalent to criminality and subject to the ultimate penalty, death.

Prey

Days of reflection; graying, growing, knowing, aging; O.G. raging, prices paid, agreements made, ideal time, rainbow cascade. Intermixed present, future and past, desolate space; takes us to an unknown place.

Once, youth obscure, no certainties, nothing for sure. Where would he go? What could he be? Questions without answers, visions to see, of far, far away and so different from me: Mom tried to understand: things she never believed, heretical thoughts barely conceived.

Places in time that doesn't exist; a time, measured with no event. So to make history of past, present true, what must one do? Can't consent to what you don't understand; to boy becoming man. And one certainly, won't consent to being prey, in a society that hunts every single day.

Will the hunted become the hunter, visions of a new way? Not in this lifetime, not in the U.S.A. "We've always hunted them." White man did say.

It's a part of living, it's just our way." "We hunt them day and night," Said the Po-Po man, "Anytime we can. It's only chinks, spics and niggers, not real men."

"Prey is what they are; prey they'll always be, doesn't mean a dam thing to a white man you see."

Juvenile probation in elementary school, no serious infraction, breaks any little rule; will keep that probation going through middle and high school. Bingo! He's 18 now, "We really got this fool."Welcome to adult probation, 'three strikes' will do; Juvenile misdeeds, at least one strike for you.

Hanging with family and friends; you've known since birth and kindergarten; oops they're felons that makes strike number two.

Almost there, where modern slaveholders want you to be; take that beer from the store shelf and make it strike number three.

So, you're now facing the end game; end of your strife? You just turned 19, and with three strikes; they got you for life. Another one caged, confused, enraged. "It's not fair." He says; "It can't be like that."

"Don't be such a victim; don't use the race card" he's told. "Maybe it's time you open your eyes brotha, and see where you at."

Two Beers: Standing in an upscale store in the well-to-do part of town, I couldn't help but notice the two homeless people in line ahead of me. I was impressed with their strength, dignity, patience, and love for each other.

Two Beers

He, just past 70, taut and lean, like ancient twine,
standing there together, she approaching

69.

Both holding furtively purchased Budweiser's,
counting quarters and dimes. Ageless is the vision
sweet love so

sublime.

She only sees his eyes, close, gently holding the
other hand: Perpetual

man.

Together, in the midst of bourgeois Long's; he
observant, cautiously waiting, anticipating, the
harshness of the

throng.

Her blue, blue eyes, innocent as youth, beam an
unwavering joy, bringing pause to the callous, the
uncouth.

Eyes tell the story, as they focus on the man. Love
transcends poverty, homelessness, sickness,
hopelessness and

crime.

Each to the other, one to another, touching all the

time.

Ever: Is about the need for that lurking truth; thankfully, often withheld, so that we can keep on doing what we do. It's also about civility, restraint and various other things making it possible for us to live and work together in this variegated societal mix that is America.

Ever

Ever got so close, knowing you'd be singed? Ever kept on pushing when every feeling told you to stop; just kept on going, knowing misfortune was your inevitable lot?

Ever wished you'd paused, knowing all you know, and refusing to stay home, when you knew you shouldn't go? Ever push, and push harder to win a tight race, knowing the power was there to keep you in your place?

Ever slept with your suspicion, held her close, touched her hand; smiled at her poison, knowing she'll kill you when she can? Ever granted a common courtesy, when you should have extended a fist; shook that offered hand, when you should have given it a twist?

Ever question words, often loosely said, knowing they'd come back to grab you, with unexpected dread? Ever wanted to take it all down, no longer pretend, and let 't he chips fall', honestly again?

Ever wonder what it's like, looking at people when they're dead; like the ones you pass in the hall that you don't see at all? Not to be interacted with, got to be dead, at least in the confines of your head.

Dead is the reality of the things we don't see, unlike you and me. Why must we see, those so called 'real' things, those meant to be?

Ever wonder why it's so hard to distinguish between, what could be and what we see; between what is you and what is me; between what is thine and what is mine; between what we believe and what we conceive; between heartfelt emotion and reactive commotion; between where you're going and where you're at; between tears of love and body sweat?

What you don't like, just say so: Kindness can hide daggers as you well know. Take it down another notch; I don't know you, you don't know me. We both like that; let it be. No more pretend or hanging around, work done, separate ways; off the grounds.

No more, "Good morning. Hello or goodbye." My greatest joy is you out of my eye.

Saturday Run In October-Neemie: October 30, 2000 was the one year anniversary of the saddest day of my life. I went for a run on that day as I did most days. Here, I speak to that run and anniversary. Years pass but the pain does not. I cried when I wrote it and I cry when I read it. Joseph Naeem "Neemie" was my son who died at age 19.

Saturday Run In October-Neemie

California sunshine, a day like any other; long run past new houses, rusting factories; new parks and old dogs, to the railroad tracks: Unlike the hills and woods of runs long ago, in that northern place of beauty where I no longer go.

Another zip code, another life, another family, another time that was mine: Where are they now, that unlikely four; scattered to the winds of grief, who raps on every door.

Death anniversary! Two huddled together, maybe someplace in LA; the other, alone as always on this melancholy day. Thoughts are of those two together, ultimately so alone, with their uniquely special memories of the brother and son gone.

Who'd dare think a number, from four to three, would mean so much to anyone, would mean so much to me. I know he watches, watches over us all; loving and praying for us, as we stumble; as we fall.

Seeing the suffering, the pain and loss; the many sleepless nights as we tumble and toss. As our lives move into new found places, he's wondering why, and what happened, to those comfortable old faces.

Whatever the circumstance he finds us in, he knows we'll love and miss him, until we meet again.

Jesse Jackson: Is about a brief encounter I had with Jesse Jackson, who until that meeting, had been one of my heroes from the civil rights movement, which I had witnessed, and lived. I had a similar meeting with Angela Davis, I introduced myself and told her what an honor it was to meet her as she grunted and kept walking past; but, yeah;; that's another story.

Jesse Jackson

Early 1970's it must have been, quite a while ago, way back when. When we were two of a few, non football playing Black men, there at USC; where on this day, Jesse Jackson chose to be.

Jesse was the man who walked beside Martin. On TV we'd seen, the blood, dogs and Billy clubs; as we watched them contend, with the violence and hatred of angry white men. Why, Jesse was standing there, on the balcony, of that very motel, the Lorraine, at Martin's end.

So, now here he was at USC. Jesse and his traveling companion, at the front of the room: presenting his 'White folks give me money speech.' He suddenly became uncomfortable as we walked in, not sure how to act, casting inexplicable, "What you doing here nigger?" hateful looks, at we two Blacks watching from the back.

Why was he angry at us, because we could see through his money for white guilt game? Get a job Jesse, this hustle is to obviously phony and lame!

How could we have known that Jesse and others'
ride on 'White guilt,' especially after the murder of
Martin, would continue for decades, a lifetime?
But, then is that guilt thing a part of who, we are as
Americans too?

Gypsies: My friend managed hotels. As we traveled she'd often point out people in various places, in a negative manner, who she called "Gypsies". Having been introduced to Gypsies only through literature and as a historian I'd ask, "How do you know that person is a Gypsy?" She'd say, "Just look at them!" I looked and saw no distinguishing characteristics. Choosing the less complicated and more simplistic viewpoint, I accused her of being racist against Gypsies. This is what I wrote from her Gypsy observations.

Gypsies

Wander Gypsy wonder, no future or past, wonder Gypsy wander, only your present will last. What happens today, no plan for tomorrow: A painless future, no present sorrow.

Wonder as you wander, with an uncommon rule, no morning wakeup or first day of school. To never see a textbook, never be late, for the inside of a Kindergarten, or grades one through eight.

Wander Gypsy wonder, ever lost in time; never solving the mysteries between grades twelve through nine. No educational keys to unlock the mind, no teachers ever, to mold, shape or refine.

Wonder Gypsy wander, nobody's fool, no time to tarry in a place called school. Take what you can, work for no man. No J-O-B for a good credit base, a stolen identity is easily replaced. Use the credit card fast, and then throw it away. Just 'get over' tonight, tomorrow's a new day.

Wander Gypsy wonder; never own a home, no house payment, or that Quicken loan.

Must rest soon; sleep where you are, a rest stop, or stolen credit card rented room. Highway rest stop, avoiding sleepless gloom, but it doesn't measure up to a Marriott's room. Use the credit card there, what can they say, "We don't serve Gypsies" that's not the American way.

Stolen card, do the credit, take what you see; flow through the 'culture', a reality that can't be. You, not knowing how to live, eat, sleep, talk, or be free: Looking into your eyes, I see, you want to be a Gypsy just like me.

Cousin Bobby: Bobby, Bobby, Bobby. Unfortunately many of us have relatives much like cousin Bobby, with whom we must interact because they are FAMILY! My cousin Bobby is possibly the most irritating person with whom I must interact. Here are a few reasons for the irritation and the interaction.

Cousin Bobby

Bobby Watkins is the only man I know, who enthusiastically, embraces failure, a life trophy he's proud to show. Now 60 years old, at family gatherings I've heard Bobby proudly say, "In my whole life, I never worked on any job, a single day."

I tactfully, suggested to Bobby that having had no job, career or life goals wasn't necessarily something to brag about. He said I was just jealous, "Cuz don't hate; cause you don't know how to get disability, welfare, food stamps or Section 8."

In another conversation, with his kids listening in, Bobby proudly told us that jail, not college, is where we find most Black men. Not true, but Bobby, rationalizing again; I reminded him that he got the loan money for college; never paid it back and chose not to attend. But jail, many times he's been.

Goggling on my phone the numbers of jailed vs. college attending Black men I showed how ridiculous his assertion had been; Bobby said, "Google is a tool used by boot licking Blacks created by racist white men!"

OOOOOOOOOOOOOOOOOOOOk.

Cousin Bobby came by to visit during the holidays; I checked the silverware before he left; because I know his ways. Realizing I was new to apartment living, cuz helpfully told me that I should hide a key outside, in case I got locked out. He even suggested a great spot.

A few days later, on the door I found a note from Cousin Bobby; reckon he dropped by to see; the spot where thankfully, I didn't hide my apartment key.

    Love you cuz, after all, you're family!

2013- Downtown: I recently, aged up, or down☺, from runner to walker. Bad knees, bad hip, and back, made running impossible. Walking the streets of this city I've noticed the varieties of folk out before sunrise. The largest early morning group is homeless, in all of life's varieties. Most will ignore you, except for a few aggressive types; sensing weakness such as; age, frailty, fear or other handicaps become takers.

2013- Downtown

Before sunrise, my walk begins, in a central
California coastal city, three miles to its end: Past
the cars of all night sleepers; morning creeps and
daylight peepers. Some, car lights on stopped at no
stop sign; passenger side door open, hoping some
careless fool will walk in.

Night denizens of modern cities, homeless eyes;
weary, alert, careless, cautious, hostile, mean:
Colorless, unmatched, under or oversized clothes;
mostly, unclean. Warily, with day breaking
footsteps, I ease past the common strife; habitually
scrutinizing doorways, alleys, benches, heating
vents, hedges, trees, and other life.

He came upon me fast, silent, soundless and on my
left side. By the time I felt presence and turned to
see, his 6'4, 250 pound frame was much too close
for neutrality. Obviously, the big fellow had done
this before, but now, he didn't know what to say,
as I turned quickly to face him, waiting for his play.

As he looked closely at each of my hands, holding eight pound weights, I realized why he paused to reconsider. "Those things could hurt somebody," he said. I agreed, still measuring the distance, of the swing to his head. Now walking alongside me, he introduced himself, and asked, "Where you from?" I did the same. Tony from New York had been in Cali for eight years, mostly in prison.

Now, he wants to go home, but his stay has been extended, he can't leave until his parole is ended. Conversation now, an easy flow; until Tony, stopping and pointing to a place on the sidewalk near the curb said: "This is my spot." We shook hands goodbye; as I had another two miles to go.

New York City: Like San Francisco, Hollywood, Los Angeles, New Orleans, Miami, Seattle, Chicago and other such places, carry an identity stamp, and models for the United States of America. All are those rare yet commonplace communities that may help complete ones understanding of who we are as a people; a nation.

New York City

Pity, such wanton beauty in that place; locked
forever in one's mental

space.

An existence felt in the minds of all; hearts
reaching out watching the towers

fall.

New York America; the essence of what we be, told
in the streets by what we hear and

see.

No unfathomable riddles, it's all out there: Look
sisters and brothers as our souls are laid

bare.

Love or hate; it matters not, if the truth be told, It's
the best that we've

got.

On This Earth: A Prayer: Here in the 21st century where many white folk, are quick to claim that we live in a post-racist era. One does wonder about the judgment of those never exposed to institutional racism. Any person of color who would dare to disagree is said to be "Using the race card" or being the victim. In a victimless society women and men of color continue fighting the daily battle at work, school and in their communities.

On This Earth

On this earth within this week, help me Lord find the things I seek; that peace of mind that comes with righteous use of time. Help me find the stability, to balance against hostility and threats to be. Help keep 'the eagle' from my door; I give him some, but he always wants more.

Help keep the neo-fascist haters, in their limited psycho-physical space; as they continue to dream and bumble harmlessly, in their world of supreme grace.

Keep the PO-PO's (Police) and the other allies of the aforementioned guys; under enough restraint to protect our lives. Help me maneuver through those mine fields, on any given day, avoiding the pitfalls of unsuspecting prey.

Remind me be watchful, as I cross the avenue; knowing some angry about his burnt toast breakfast white man; may decide that I'm Iraqi too.

Help me avoid those fools with whom I work, and their twisted movie/television stereotyped view, of what a Black man is supposed to say think and do. Give me the strength to model in every way, the conduct of a caring citizen of an unbiased republic; day, after day, after day.

Together we must take that chance; get out there and work it; participate in the dance. Whatever it may be; step up or down; even swing a partner around. Dip and swirl, twist and curl. Finally, give us the strength to say: "My voice, my choice; I participate in my own way; my life, mine alone; every Day."

 Help me teach the opposite, of the things I experience and see, directed at people of poverty and color, in this society. Give me strength to ignore the ironic contradictions, and to make a better place for those who follow me and you. A better world, un hip; square; squeaky clean; that is the hope; that is the dream: Yep, the bottom line; maybe, that's what it all means.

III

Snake Tail: This tale is from the days of chopping cotton during the early 1960''s in Arkansas, and of daily looking forward to turning 18 and leaving those fields behind.

Snake Tail

A spotted brown circle in the stillness, dozing, as he waited: knotty tail, lying quietly; slightly long, now, horizontally. Friend Charles and I, 'Running our mouths' about futures far, far, from here, chopping cotton with our hoes, moving inexorably near. Near. Nearer to spotted brown, recumbent, in the shade of the cotton stalks, on the cool ground.

Why do we talk, on and on endlessly, about a future life we hope to see? Maybe we too live by the saying: "To survive where you are and the pain you see, look to the future and the joy to be. Joy to be is not a thing you just find. Joy to be comes from a passionate mind."

Meanwhile, snake waits.

I looked at Charles as he moved up the row, keeping a good pace, chopping real slow: So many things to discuss, among those cotton stalks much taller than us. The places we'd go; and the cars we'd drive to jobs where we'd thrive: Beautiful home, comfortable life, a place far away, with a beautiful wife.

Meanwhile, snake waits.

We wondered how to get out of those fields, and to things, only the future would show? So much in our heads as we chopped Mr. Knox's cotton, bouncing off our lips before they're forgotten: It was all out there, waiting for us to grow, into that life we'd someday know.

Meanwhile, snake waits.

Dark green cotton stalks, light green grass, brown dirt underfoot as we began to chop fast. Now, growling stomachs, breakfast didn't last. I asked Charles if his future wife would be fine, he said, "I don't know about yours, but mine will be fine."

Meanwhile, snake waits.

Hot Arkansas day was like many others, with Charles and I 'riding' those chopping hoes, together like brothers. He back turned, moving down the row, while I facing forward was chopping conventionally as we go.

Meanwhile, snake waits.

Charles was telling me about his future house, the 2nd floor stairway, and circular round, when I saw a flicking tongue, small head, moving up and down; a knobby vertical tail making a clicking sound. The rattlesnake was big, three or four years old, open mouth, head back, to wreak havoc untold.

Right foot coming down; my shout stopped him mid-stride: One jump, took Charles past me: As I hit the rattlesnake, he landed on my opposite side.

The drama over before a good start, with the
snake, below the cotton stalks, now in several
parts.

Meanwhile...

Charles' wife and three children became very real,
in a future that the snake tried to steal.

Hawk: Tells the story of a bird that I'd become used to seeing on the farms and fields of the south, and in the hills and forests of California. However, standing on a street corner during a break; amongst the skyscrapers and bumper to bumper traffic in 'The City', I happened to glance up at a nearby light post. To my surprise there as was I; calmly surveying the chaotic human scene, sat a most beautiful hawk.

Hawk

O' mighty hawk, I'm surprised to see your face, on this lamppost in 'The City'; it seems so out of place. What can you hunt here? What do you see, high on your metal post above this concrete eternity? Are there field mice in "The City": Are you getting fat, or must you now choose and urban rat? Is he harder to handle, this streetwise prey? Do you wrestle and fight him, or just fly away?

What is your food source in this compendium of steel, so far, far away, from the once open fields? Is Colonel Sanders' garbage where you now take your meals? Was that gliding, soaring, diving free hawk that we once knew, a vision of a past we feel, or glimpse of a present unreal, where he lives happily, amongst the crowds of steel?

I remember a time, not so long ago, when places like this, we didn't want to know. With limitless vision, as far as the eye could see, tree green horizons, beckoned you and me. I running hard, and jumping so high, hawk, soaring easily across a faded blue sky. Things were different then, and so were we, headed for changes, steeped in profundity; neither could foresee.

Now, here; with the baggage of what we felt, and what we feel, ensconced in this abyss, of concrete and steel. Our days and all our ways, wrapped in serenity, steeped in the secrecy, called individuality. What we do, what we say, is but the life experience of one more day.

Alive, living, in our own way: Because it's good for you, is it good for me too? Sista Hawk; be thoughtful, with caution, and watch what you do. Join in love and caring, with other creatures of this sea and land. Live well in the joy of this new place, as our worlds expand.

Light: Examines the question of whether our emotions, feelings, attitudes and overall demeanor; are determined by the change from light to darkness or darkness to light? Is that Jekyll –Hyde personality, though oftentimes minute, in all of us; decided by the shadings of light and darkness?

Light

Sun swept day, clear, clear bright, California colors, fantastic sight. Cali-Day beauty, Cali-Day light, sadly watch it fade, with the coming night. Steal a bit of beauty, with man-made light. Push away the darkness, bright the way I see, man-made vision lights the way for me.

When there is light in the darkness, shadows in the night, there is no real dilemma, just roll with the light. I do wonder; if she loved me in the gloom, will she still in the light? If she lied to me this morning, will she speak true tonight? Does light make a difference, in **what** we do and say? Is the **when** most important for the words we speak each day?

Is sunshine most reflective of feelings of joy; making every mood and action luminescent as we grow, covered by its warm, vitamin enriched glow? What about the darkness, of Cali-Night, does what we say then, mean less than words of Cali-Light? Do words have less might, if spoken at night?

So, what words are best for use during day? What of anger, hate, and deceit; are they only for day say? Gentle true and loving; are they just tight for

night? Sun ray direction, earth rotations,
reflections; moon shadow bisections; night or day
one should   consider, before saying that word you
were going to say.

Tree: Standing just outside of a collection of office building in a suburban northern California city stood a lone redwood tree, the final remnant of a once burgeoning forest. You couldn't help but notice it, as it was the only tree of its size within miles.

Tree

Shadowing a wall, more than just lumber; Gods giant creature, stands sixty feet tall. Straight, cool, green; redwood trunk, limbs reaching, tinged red gold; beauty to behold. Leafy smells slide discreetly up your nose. Roots go deep, almost straight down; tap water, far underground.

Atop, sits the raven, surveying his domain; circling squawking Blue Jays add an auditory refrain. All in hyperspace, high altitude sound; lives a hard beaked community; rarely looking down. Birds, humans, trees: all pretty much the same; forever locked in and disagreeing over territorial gain.

Is the tree a part of you and me? "Damm right it is!" We are all wrapped up, in this same earthly cup. Alive with a responsibility, to protect and respect all life, even the highly tree: God's living creature like you, like me.

Santa Rosa Life-ANNADELL: Is a story about one of the most beautiful running trails I've ever run, which I ran daily. On this day the run was most unforgettable.

Santa Rosa Life – ANNADELL

In those hills, the places I go, thankful to God for the beauty I know. Things I see so fine to me, as simple as a bird or leaf on a tree. Birds so brown, yellow, blue, and other hues for run past views. One more mile in this beauty enveloped dust, one more step, tirelessly I must.

Redwoods, tall sentinels they are, as I peer through their trunks, at the lake below afar. Lake Ilsanjo waits; around the next corner, the next bend; anticipatory vision, I took it all in. If I take the short cut down, an ankle twisting drop, of thick brush and broken rock; recumbent rattlesnakes chomping at my hocks, I'd be at Ilsanjo in a mile or two.

However, the long way down, Is less profound, and safer too. Yesterdays grass field seemed a little bit greener, and today's wild turkey flock, 200 strong,; crowds the trail sounding disturbingly meaner. Sitting on the big rock above the fog enshrouded city, brought simple words to mind, like beauty and pretty.

Ten miles behind me, to rest for a minute; another challenging Annadell run, thank God I'm still in it. Bad knees, bad back, bad ankles too; but keep on running, that's what I do. I run in a space that clarifies reality; with rocks, leaves, flowers, grass, golden dust, gnats, an even a recalcitrant bee.

The woman on the horse waved as they plodded past. I gave a hand in return from my comfortable nest.

Euphorically, gazing behind her on the trail, I saw a tawny brownish creature, swishing its tail. Moving ever purposely, head hanging down, shoulder muscles flexing, up and circle round. Silent feet sank into the dust, claws to the ground.

Motionless, I watched him thinking, "He looks like. Odie." As the big cat froze, staring, with fixed yellow eyes. "Not my housecat Odie," I thought with surprise. What do I do now, do men scream? There stood a real mountain lion, whose pictures, I'd only seen.

Swishing tail, yellow eyes, looking at me; I was looking back, knowing that creature, was about to attack. Finding anger and determination, rising from the rock to a standing position, I carefully moved, eyeing his hard bunched muscles; and waited for him to choose.

He must have been very hungry, looking for easy prey, but I felt it, deep in my heart, partner, "I ain't dying today! Watching his poised immobility, gauging his weight and size, I saw his shoulders flex and thought, he has chosen, and this is where he dies.

Four eyes locked, staring; he leapt in a slow rush.
Fluidity of motion is a description that came to
mind as he landed on the rocks above me,
disappearing into the red dust and brush.

 Breathing hard, standing there, thinking, this has
got to be a dream; but the broken brush and lion
tracks, brought reality to the scene.

I continued my run that morning, and I still run
those hills, but nowadays, I restrict myself, to the
smaller plants and animals, for daily visual thrills.

Drive: This story tells of a place I drove past numerous times on my trips home to visit my mom; from Northern California to Arkansas on US Highway 40. From the start, I'd drive non-stop as far as I could without rest. After the first time, of which I here write, I noticed that when at the absolute end of my endurance; when I couldn't go one mile further; I'd find myself at this most unusual rest stop.

Drive

After eight hundred miles of US Highway 40 East a
place to rest was a critical quest: Finally
somewhere in Texas, a rest stop. In its circular ring,
the desolate stillness, I felt; very first thing. Thin
leafless trees; with limbs extended skyward; like
featherless bird wings. Were they reaching for the
heavens above or pulling from the hell below? Only
God and Satan know.

Two vehicles on the grounds: An engineless rusting
pickup truck, and a car; without windows or
wheels; both axles broken down. No bathrooms,
drinking fountains or other buildings I'd come to
know; here, just dirt clods and tumbleweeds,
where lawn would normally grow.

Observations from exhaustion, as I began to doze;
hands on the Walther PPK trigger underneath my
clothes. Though feeling a strong sense of danger,
sometimes you just 'know', but I'd been nodding
off at the wheel; not one mile further could I go.

Asleep in minutes, not a whimper or dream; off into nothingness, blanket covered scene.

Later, a heavy, heavy feeling; deep in sleep; pressing hard on the car; the air; my body and the seat. Waiting, powerful, unfulfilled hatred; unreasonable without attachment; unrestrained; mean, mean!

There was nothing to touch or see; as the oncoming dread, fear, disaster; was overwhelming, unstoppable; meant to be. Faceless, though I felt a deathly staring vision; no body to be seen; incomprehensible strength; muscular precision.

No hands did I see; but felt hostile appendages, reaching out for me. Laying there, afraid to sleep or to wake up; touched by incoherent thinking; negative power from an overflowing cup.

Confused, wondering what, how: When the strongest urge, said: "If you want to live, get out of here, leave now!" Didn't need a second telling; action uncompromising; rolling from that rest stop while the automatic seat was still rising.

I remain, thankful to God today, as I was thankful then, for stepping in to save this life; once again; once again.

I Saw Him: Have you ever been so low that you lived only because your body doggedly, kept functioning; so low that on your daily drive to work you had this back and forth debate with yourself, trying to decide whether to turn the car head-on into an oncoming semi. I Saw Him is from some of the hardest times and the beginning of a positive turnaround. This also was a time of some very heated discussion with 'the big fellow', God.

I Saw Him

At some time in our lives we reach that point of which we know, we don't wish to go. Wallowing in the ensuing pity and wondering, how you got to that earthen hell; when just yesterday you were doing so well. Yesterday; perfect job, perfect pay, perfect woman, children, accoutrements made for a perfect day.

Today, lying on a too small twin bed; tiny apartment; alone, jobs gone, woman too; what do I do? What happened to me; what are the things that caused this to be? The death of a child: God I miss him, he's gone, what to do; what do I do? Feeling that overwhelming end, inexcusably, I left the family too.

Now, no family, no wife; I am but just another jobless man with no life. Life? To top off the overwhelming negativity; high blood pressure numbers, were amazing to see. Heights unheard of with life: 200/290, 185/270, 206/295 and driving to Emergency, again and again.

There, to take a seat in room number one; waiting with the medics for the stroke to come. Waiting over; when the blood vessel finally popped; the medic quipped, "No stroke, it's just a little bit high." Lucky me, just blinded in one eye.

Somewhere between sleep and wakefulness, back home in bed, I said to God, "You took my friends, my marriage, my family, my job, and my son's life; my sight, and brought such strife; why not take my life? "As I continued my mental bickering, arguing with Him; a vision began to unfold.

 Suddenly, I felt I was looking through a camera lens, slowly panning a scene, wondering: "Is this a dream?" With much, much historical detail, connecting time and place, a realism and clarity; clear enough to touch.

I saw the muscular back of a man, sitting on a Roman bench, wearing a Toga, draped over one shoulder, with the other exposed.

No words exchanged; I knew this man was Jesus. Didn't think it the least odd or strange, that I was having a speechless argument with a man who died more than 2,000 years ago; the son of God, Jesus Christ; and saying with great hostility, "You've done all those awful things to me, including taking my son, and now you've taken sight from my left eye!"

During the heavy silence, I stared hard at his clothes, his back, and the sculpted linear detail of the Roman Bench on which he was sitting, unti I he wordlessly responded: "At least you got one eye."Within the following long pause, I started to laugh.

Awakening from the vision/dream I was laughing, laughing for the first time in a very long while. It felt good! So began the road to recovery, with a laugh, which brought a restoration of hope and purpose. Grinning to a new beginning☺

No Fear: Reflects my change in attitude toward life and living; following my encounter with God. I know it may sound odd to some, so crazy they may not read beyond this chapter, but it is what it is.

No Fear

Brings arrogance about those things one knows,
empowering knowledge, the secret never shows.
Though wanting to yell from the rooftops, shine in
a magic glow, for all to see; high and low.

Go on each day moving inexorably through here;
with no trepidations, walk without fear.

When confronting mean people in that bad place,
as hatreds angry hand reaches for your face: Slap it
aside and maintain your own pace.

God's grace; your source of mental and physical
power; be pleased and absolutely certain, that he is
with you every second, every hour. Never asking,
"Which way?" as he guides us every day.

Never questioning where, or fearing what you see,
remembering, so long as God is with you; you're
where you are supposed to be.

Twinkle Me: A response, with a slight bite, to information overload and the evening news, now 24/7 on any station any day.

Twinkle Me

Dear Lord have mercy as you hear what I say; and help me through this second, minute, hour; this one more day.

Surviving by example, moving from one to the next; the more we try to fix it the more ephemeral it gets.

Get, get away from here; is it happening everywhere? Is just around the corner still far away from there?

Twinkle me, twinkle me; help me spread the light; twinkle me, twinkle me; before day turns to night.

Twinkle me, twinkle me; show me the way; twinkle me, twinkle me; hear what I say.

Say, has the world lost its way? Daily we witness, fratricide, matricide, patricide, and infanticide on the news; repetitiously; glorified.

Christians kill Moslems; Moslems killing Christians; Moslems and Christians killing Hindus, Moslems and Sikhs. What must we do: They are killing animals too?

Arabs are killing in the name of Allah; Jews and Christians in the name of Yahweh and all in the name of God.

Twinkle me, twinkle me; bring the new day; twinkle me, twinkle me; make it all go

away.

Hottie: I worked with this very attractive woman who enjoyed the attention bestowed upon her by students, me, and other male workers at the school. This writing comes from my observations on a day that we sat outside together during break.

Hottie

Broken leaf drying on a table tin hot; with edible fruit, garlic: Maybe not. Cup on the table, metallic green; wedding planner book, it's clear what that means. Another good man finds a great wife; together forever, a brand new life.

Cell phone upside down, waiting for the call to bring us around: Here, sunglasses, not being worn, prop lying in the shade, unnecessary thorn. Gucci purse, sits, poised and refined, on the cold scratched table; subtle, sublime.

High maintenance woman, leans back in her chair; long brown legs, flapping in the air: Fine, fine distraction, on this cloudless fall day; here for a little while, then she goes away.

Not for me, or any of these hounds, tall diamonds on her finger, notice to clowns. Previously taken! She just wants to play.

Her: The search may be a lifetime task in which we touch many others and share a bit of pain. At the time 'she' was all encompassing, mastering all aspects of life as I knew it. But doubt, such a spoiler, as it often does, began to slowly creep in.

Her

Melancholy, hanging in the air, following through the day here and there: What happened to the lightness, the fun? Joyless days and nights are not worth the run. Run, running everywhere; does it mean anything if you really don't care? Show me a smile; a grin; that you care whether I'm out or in.

Show that bounce, the confident swagger, without deceit; no unsheathed dagger. Openness, clear days blue sky, good, good feelings, brightness of eye. The eyes say it, truth or lie, window to the heart, looks closely; don't cry. Memories of days holding each other near; should take the tears far from here.

Never bring the water; dripping from the eye, making all who see it, sympathetically sigh. See the flash, mark the speed, corral the joy, feed the need. Let's do this! Make it right! Forget the darkness, leave the night. Pursing the dream, quite enough for me; withholding judgment, I'll wait and see.

Lines: Aging, growing old is that monster who wreaks havoc upon our bodies; havoc we notice more in others than ourselves. In others no glancing looks, full critique, especially if it's someone, like a former girlfriend or an ex wife, who you've known and loved since the days of youthful beauty.

Lines

Just below the eyes, tear made gullies, cutting deep inside. On both cheeks, the lines burrow; making chins, jowls; and on the forehead a deep, deep furrow. Twisted lines moving on a white deck, blue veins tracing a crooked neck.

Lines gazing at the face, remembering our pasts, how many did I place? Years of joy, recent pain, happiness fades; new reality reigns. Mind began to wander, remembering when, looking at the now, wishing for the then.

It was so very bright, touchily near, not of today, memories, oh so clear. Silky fine surfaces were rounded and smooth, so sensuously tight, before oncoming night. Empathize, sympathize be nostalgic of kind, cellulite of body, cellulite of mind. Keep on moving.

No recovery time, sorrow for the sadness, or sympathy for the pain, faded pictures will never live again. If only we could re do, different I say I'd be; a model of decorum, love and sensitivity.

Today, I see your smile, hear the vocal sounds, am overwhelmed by the pain, of the lines your face surrounds. Focus on the eyes, where I see, the hue of youth, looking back at me.

Reminiscent curiosity, restrained shadows of care, hiding behind the blue: Will I ever come back here? I wish I knew.

Yellow Eyed White Girl: Briefly chronicles an event from another part of that lonely time living in Walnut Creek, an East Bay city in Northern CA.

Yellow Eyed White Girl

Yellow eyed girl, looking at me. Yeah, a Black man,
like what you

see?

Across the centuries, I look back, more immediate
past, from across the

track.

You see your, present, your time. I too see events,
exclusively

mine.

So our pasts are different, does it matter today?
"Damm right it does, when Black men are prey!"

Prey in this state of ancient structure based on
sexual dread. If I followed the road you offer, I'd
soon be dead.

Yellow eyes inviting, so are your pouty lips; shapely
legs; fine chest and slightly flaring

hips.

Intelligence behind the eyes, mirroring the mind, which just may not be as important, as your well stacked behind.

Black values slipping, the power of a glance; outdated prohibition,

interracial romance.

Some may fashionably pretend, within the white chatter; stereotypical trends, housing ins and media manipulations of minority situations, it really doesn't matter.

But looking at you again, Ms. Polly Ann, I must say, "Black man is prey," as I walk far, far

away.

Clack, Clack, Clack: The sound of her shoes was the first thing I noticed about her, and the last.

Clack, Clack, Clack

Silence filled room, won't answer the door, companionship gone, don't need it anymore. Telephone rings, I listen to the sound; if no one answers no one is around. Movie on Friday, parked at Longs, beside a blond in a Range Rover, well built and strong.

Crossing at the light, a whiff of perfume; sweet, sweet scents, penetrates my gloom. Slowing down for a hesitant pass, I wanted to speak; as I watched her fine ass.

Paths crossed again in the ticket line, me so nervous; she so fine. Close enough to smell her one more time. What about a date? We're both here alone, act right now, before her essence is gone.

Perchance meeting in this time and place, to respond to, or ignore the feelings, remaining locked in our personal space. Is loneliness out of bounds of decorum and responsibility, transcending race and gender credibly?

Eyes slate grey, turned to stare at me, looking back in return, afraid of what I see: Honesty, hope, fear and pain; withdrawing into myself, a silent remain:

Watching beauty walk away in shoes going clack, clack, clack; sitting alone in the theatre, way in the back.

Shine On: I was thinking about 'her' while 'she' was out shopping and scribbled this little ditty. It was just another incomplete attempt to describe the indescribable uniqueness of feelings that most often are called love. Looking at the date of this writing I was able to place the person connected to those feelings and I wonder; "Did I really feel that way about her?"

Shine On

Sometimes gray sometimes blue; varieties of the spectrum shine, reflecting complexity of mind;

and body too, in the constantly changing vision of the light that is

you.

At times so bright, blinding to see; in the master glow I asked, "Is it you, or is it

me?"

When the light was low, I struggled in the dark; waiting for the glimmer, waiting for the

spark.

Soon to come, bringing relief and joy, to the man who loves you and his inner

boy.

Lose-Lose: Sometimes, through no fault of our own, we just can't win. Trying hard to control our own situations, we soon discover that we have absolutely no say in the lives and decisions of others, regardless of how close they are or claim to be. The most we can do is put it all out there and pray for reciprocity.

Lose-Lose

Unspoken promises, at the beginning, faded memories, added time, when we heard that song he was singing "...always on my mind..." added lines to the story, a lifetime sang, as we traveled different places, new alliances; other faces. Heretofore, words unspoken, the depth of the feel, never minimized, the power of the real.

Then we added more vocals to the mix; creating a complexity we two couldn't fix. Experience, adversity and time, life's subtleties and grind; foreshadowing a present, that would never be mine. Took me places, I'd never been, an open doorway, I rarely get in. Leading me to depths, I'd never seen, holding me so very close, a drugless dream.

With my hand, I touched the center of your soul. Such overwhelming trust left me humble, angst filled, foreboding and cold. Cold with a future foreseeable, a whisper in my ear: "What a joy to walk with her and for the longest moment, hold her near" Mental and physicality to fine to flaunt; she came to me, saying; "Do what you want."

Our vertiginous perceptions, lifetime of dreams, were shaped in the reality of this emotio-intellectual scheme.

Imagine timeless beauty, forever by her side; psychosomatose sharing, two volcanoes, life balance abide. Together, knowledge and strength to burn a path across the land, shared loving and caring to warm the hearts of man.

A future of tinkering, fixing all we see; open hearts touching; me to you, you to me. Nothing, can I do here but dream. It doesn't matter the words used or what she may say. Doesn't matter whether she speaks true; or the happiness I feel, as we touch each other every conceivable way.

Stolen moments with a Black man, memory fading with every step, as she slowly walks away: To her life as a White woman in a White world, where she will stay. Thus the ultimate point of silence, peers deep within my soul, to see her asleep on the bed of another, with whom she has chosen to grow old.

Joslyn: Was a friend of friends who happened to be visiting, as was I, their home for Thanksgiving when we met. I was too old, 50's and she was too young, 20's, and not really interested in many folk outside of herself. This, my friend Rosie knew, and tried to warn me, but I ignored her wise counsel.

Joslyn

Such a good feeling, a holiday, seeing the familiar
faces; all a bit older now, and wiser about the eyes;
showing hints of the year's successes, failures and
tries. On this day of Thanksgiving, among family
and friends, all is well in God's world, amen, amen.

Out of the corner of an eye, moving through the
crowd, I noticed a beautiful stillness, silently aloud.
Observing that face, discreetly from the side, I felt
her critical concentration, enveloping kids, adults
and all things inside. Listening, aware of the
situational surround, she took it all in without a
participatory sound.

What she sees and hears; beauty listening behind
the words, seeing beyond the ears. Sitting she is a
pleasurable sight; when standing, is this too true?
The question was immediately answered, as I could
plainly see the shapely body as she walked past
me. Oops, I saw intelligence, tact and cunning too;
to get what she wants, she'll do what she has to
do.

Goal oriented, unquenchable thirst, all may get
what they want, but she gets hers first. Quick

impressions aside; couldn't wait to see; what kind of person she'd turn out to be. Shopping for the niece, she accompanied me, buying several pleasing things; good fun. Alone I couldn't have done.

Thankful and curious, I bought a couple of things for beauty too. Would she pass or misunderstand? Some think kindness is weakness, especially coming from a 'brother man.' Kindness too is a test, to see what the recipient will do. How is it received? It's like reading a book, watch the pages turn, take time to look.

All those things left untold, stuff that couldn't be, listen closely, and watch the truth of the person shown, on those open pages, easy to see. My friend Rosie noticed my interest and Charles did too; both told me informational stories; saying Beauty was not a thing I should do. "You have everything." Rosie said, "Young girls like that have nothing, to offer you."

"Besides, can't you see, she's like family. Our big movie date just wasn't meant to be; sweet Rosie kept me late in Lancaster, CA so Joslyn I wouldn't see. Watching her, as she told me she forgot the time, "It was an accident." she said; as she dropped her head; Rosie, wouldn't look at me.

A week later, back in my place, I was thinking daily, how nice it would be to begin my days, waking to that beautiful face. Sunday, on the phone, maybe there was a glimmer of hope a possibility. HERE: I ended this writing with the statement, "To be continued, as we move through this life; maybe with destinies joined avoiding negative discourse.

Postscript: IT NEVER HAPPENED! Thank God! Joslyn and I spent a long night together, on our third meeting, where she spelled out her conditions for a relationship. I never got past condition number one. She told me of the nice car that I was t o buy her, she'd already talked it over with the dealer, we just had to pick it up. So went the last time I saw Joslyn.

The Five-Four (54) Ballroom: The Five-Four Ballroom took its name from its location at 54th Street and Broadway Avenue in Los Angeles. Much like other clubs on the so-called 'Chitlin Circuit' located in Black neighborhoods across the country; at the 54 one could see top R&B stars for 2 or three dollars.

The Five-Four (54) Ballroom

Ruby, a beauty from Wells Bayou, Arkansas; who I'd loved back in the day, from a distance, distance because she had four older brothers, decided to visit LA.I called to say hello, and to ask her to go with me to see James Brown at the Five-Four.

The Five-Four was the weekend place to be to catch the Temptations, Supremes, Marvin Gaye; and other Black Stars of the day. This night was magic, exciting, and electric; we felt the same; seeing each other and Brother James.

At the time, I thought she and James Brown were the show; but looking back; it was always the Five-Four. The Five-Four, representative of a time unlike today, when the races in America were separate; each went their own way.

Saturday night at the Five-Four; a sea of Black faces, dressed to the nines; in the city of the Angels, where even ugly people look fine. The entrance, above the 1st floor; was at the top of the carpeted stair, a wide open door.

Men selling tickets, both were wearing ties; the smaller of the two, the bouncer; a long razor scar on his neck; no feeling in his eyes: Closer, glowing anticipation, we could see a little more; candlelit tables circling a gigantic dance floor.

But 'The Table' at the front entrance, was by far; the most memorable aspect of the Five-four: Overflowing with its unique content, rising two or three feet in the air; easily visible from the bottom stair.

Claim checks, none asked for or given: All courteously responded to the house rule: "No weapons past the door!" at the Five-Four. Laying my weapon on a corner of the table, we couldn't help but stop and stare, at the variety of objects, casually placed there.

Billy clubs, machetes, daggers, brass knuckles, short bats, Lugers, 25, 32, 38 and 45 caliber pistols; from the pockets and purses of those smiling angelic faces, filled all the table spaces.

Inside, we watched a great show, while anticipating the best performance coming afterward; as we prepared to go: The rearming of the masses at the weapons table; before leaving the

Five-Four.

Sista, Forgive my Stupidity: Catherine I met while in graduate school at USC. She was bright, subtle, exotic (Guyanese), and physically, 'turn your head' beautiful. After several months she finally agreed to go out with me. This brief comment speaks of just one amazing day with her. Soon after, foolishly, I left. Again another turn, another walk away: I've done some leaving in this life.

Sista, Forgive My Stupidity

Black, beautiful and so, so, fine...

On this mountain, atop gigantic brown rocks we

lie,

Fingers tight to each other, hands touching puffy
white clouds, slowly floating by: damp, damp
coolness of the flowing

sky.

Afro head, softly on your breast, heartbeat, and
sigh; how could I know that time, place, you; so
very special; soon to pass me

by.

Didn't know to hold the moment; the mountain;
your body; the clouds; the story searing passion:
Pillow memories on the

fly.

Yesterday, Time and Circumstance: For more than 20 years I lived north of the Golden Gate Bridge. Working in San Francisco; I crossed it daily, going to and from work. Sometimes on weekends I and the family again traveled to SF to compete in various footraces. Consequently, most of the joy in my life was spent with family, north of the Golden Gate Bridge.

Yesterday, Time and Circumstance

Once again 'The City' a part of my daily work routine. Though time and circumstance had changed, I still marveled at the continuity, of the life stream.

   Yesterday time and circumstance.

Unchanging beauty, no proper words to say; San Francisco, is always like, I was just here yesterday, yesterday,

   Yesterday; time and circumstance.

On automatic pilot, as my workday ends, with just a few hours before the new one begins: Homeward, moving through the darkness; nighttime streets again.

   Yesterday, time and circumstance.

Barely noticing the signs; shift the gears and roll, tightly closed windows; outside rain and cold.

   Yesterday, time and circumstance.

Feel it all inside, no matter what you say; every insignificant detail, moment, time and space: Shared routine of joy and sadness, in that particular place.

Yesterday, time and circumstance.

Even tiny memories, heartfelt pricks of pain, reflects a present, overflowing with past remains.

Yesterday, time and circumstance.

No I didn't notice the buildings or the cars alongside: Autopilots taking me home, I'm just along for the ride.

Yesterday, time and circumstance.

Right turn here, left there, rolling through exhaustion, black wheels taking me where...

Yesterday, time and circumstance.

A prisoner of past daytimes; weekends; holidays; growing children's entertainments, activities; associations; and timing swim relays.

Yesterday, time and circumstance.

How does time work; is it simple like in stories told? Will an act of present, erase the recent past and bring back the old? Can a present act erase what came before; mistakes be gone; and open that closed door?

Yesterday, time and circumstance.

Today, puts the clock back 'there', to a place where all, were present, all were clear; there was here!

Yesterday, time and circumstance.

All, were we, at "The House", of snug and warm, four inside; love, comfort, children, and great pride. Grades, event times, games, concerts, city councils, cars, licenses and travel to name a few: Every swim meet, every summer, every tent, hotel, motel, hot day in Napa and Luanne's rent too.

Yesterday, time and circumstance.

Hold up! Stop! The overwhelming pathos, what brought it on? Past is past, what's gone is gone!

Yesterday, time and circumstance.

Nothing we say or do will remove the pain we've gone through. We can't change what we feel or thought real.

Yesterday, time and circumstance.

The history is also here, part of the record of ours, and others pain and fear.

Yesterday, time and circumstance.

Yes, the record of our past is there to see; the years, the kids, you and me.

Yesterday, time and circumstance.

We were quite the trailblazers, a sight to behold, or so I'm told: Another story; more lines for another time.

Yesterday, time and circumstance.

Left my present digs this morning, another uneventful day; doing the things I'm supposed to do, making my way. I added five night hours and made a fourteen hour day.

Yesterday time and circumstance.

That's what I do! Work ends, next agenda item; move on; today's, finally through!

Yesterday, time and circumstance.

I didn't realize what I'd done, until I saw the first tower: The wrong bridge, wrong year, wrong day, wrong time, and wrong hour.

Yesterday, time and circumstance.

The Golden Gate; wrong door for the wrong shore: North shore, where I don't live anymore: The way to a past that didn't last, North Bay, not today or ever again.

Yesterday, time and circumstance.

So, is a tired man's lot; heading for a home that's not; not home? All has changed; though it looks the same; impenetrable barriers of past hurt remain; mental images an abatis of pain.

Yesterday, time and circumstance.

Home? Not welcome there, now the land of the enemy. Now ugly to see, the place where the most unimaginable, became the undeniable truth of me.

Avoiding the sadness of an X-home and an X-wife the North way, I made a U-Turn; heading for the right bridge to my new home in the East Bay.

Yesterday. Time and circumstance.

V

The Alternative Ed. Student: Gives one a peek at students who in many ways reflect the typicality of today's schools. But the alternative education student fills the outer edges of that majority group expected to benefit from *No Child Left Behind* and other dubious legislation.

The Alternative Ed. Student

They come; much welded, painted over, repainted, twisted, retwisted, banged, squished, pounded, crushed and bled to a point near mental and/or physical death.

Then, barely alive, they, like the shells of cars in a demolition derby, are again welded, painted, repainted, twisted, retwisted, banged, squished, pounded, crushed, bled and again pushed into the arena; and expected to perform at or above maximum capacity.

Amazingly, they do; perform much better than you or I would/could under same or similar circumstance.

One Day: Alternative education kids, many students of color and/or poverty; kicked out of the regular school programs due to gang activity, violence and/or non- attendance. Ankle bracelets; juvenile probation or parole is not uncommon. Teacher knowledge of the constantly changing gang signs and symbols; are a valuable necessity for classroom seating, safety and control.

One Day

Judging the distance I knew I couldn't stop it: The choice, to break his hand or the pencil; either he'd drop it. 'Bad blood' between them, several days flowing; loud profanities outside and in, quieted down for a minute, thought it might end.

Like a small hurricane, we watched it growing for days; hoping someone else's landfall, would sap the strength of its ways. But no, true to my fear, it was going to happen right now, right here.

Why my classroom; why me? Tiring is the petty senseless violence, as any fool could see. Carlos sat one seat in front of Waddell and off to his right; unfortunately, just far enough ahead, so Waddell was out of his line of sight.

Wishing that he'd seen it, razor sharp coming down; the #2 on the pencil, stuck in Carlos' face, as I twisted Waddell's arm and forced him down. Then checking for blood flow and shock, observing Carlos' puzzled frown, in the following deep silence; I could feel the other students, profound.

Why did he stab him, who knows? Deal with results, however it goes. Carlos bounded from his seat, books and other kids asunder, his bellow in the silence, shook the room like thunder. All were now standing, assistance; dare I ask; alone, keeping the two separate, an impossible task.

My look of desperation brought Marcelino and Jose, to hold Carlos back, while Angela called the Police to quell this new attack. Finally, the necessary things done; bodies moved here and there, blood off the desktops and floor, Police, EMTs and fighters, all out the door.

A few minutes chatter, not really much to say, and we were back to classroom events at the school called Community Day.

Teaching: Another great performance by all? Here, we pretend the most bizarre, obscene, and mean are commonplace; just a part of the 'normal' scene.

It Ain't Me: In this writing is the absolute essence of an unfortunate majority of those students finding themselves in the alternative education system.

It Ain't Me

 In this place of hostility, I must fight you, I must fight me. Ask no questions, let me be; nothing, is what I do here, it's plain to see.

I feel inadequate! I feel lost! I don't understand the words on this page! What's my age? Well I'm old enough to read. Tough? Seventeen years is that so rough?

What's the cost for lost? I want to leave, but embarrassment won't let me go; some of the words on the pages of this book I must know.

That teacher is a hater; can't you see; It ain't me! Try? Why should I? I can't do this, I already know. It's too hard; why can't I go?

"I hate this school! I hate this place; and if I wasn't on probation; you wouldn't see my face."I hate you, and 'quiet as it's kept,

'I hate me too!

Adamont School: Here is offered a description of a modern day one-room-schoolhouse in a California bay area city with an outdoor garden and other amenities.

Adamont School

Flowers, yellow, purple, white and maroon; disheveled brown haystacks; leaning against the room. Tomatoes small and green, sunflowers too; tall, tall trees; trunks colored like coffee brew.

With limbs hanging down, so very, very low; swishing in a wind ever so slow. Low was the building, in a color light to see; two squat window eyes looking at the tree.

Gray garbage can, fronting a square iron door, outside lunch table, chained to the tarmac floor.

Four foot iron fence; built in a square, enclosing plants, chairs, pots, a basketball hoop, and students attending there.

Boxes of potted jasmine, on the left fence, an aroma of climbing exotica incense. At the intersection of the four foot fence, a five foot hedge spreading wide in suspense.

Four goes to fourteen feet, with the height of the tree, in a colorful covering of flowered variety. Here again the reds, yellows, purples and blue; pink and oranges make an appearance too.

Black top yard, waiting in front: "Hello young man, welcome to Adamont."

Hoop: Much like the few people I've ever met from Indiana, both male and female; all who claimed to be excellent basketball players: Alternative education students, most often, brazenly make the same claim. Hoop was co-written by one such student.

Hoop

Round orange circle, hanging ten feet high; going
up for a jam, I almost touch the

sky.

Backboard glass, see through veneer; a light 'kiss'
off the square; two points

here.

Cotton net hanging, way up in the air, three point
jumpers; I can swish it from there.

Long black pole, flowing down from the square,
driving hard to the hoop; remember that it's

there?

Binkwitz School: Another inner city school with all of the aforementioned issues. But those issues and how manifest were unique to Binkwitz. Hopefully, a true vision of what I saw and not a vision of what I'd like to have seen.

Binkwitz School

Joyful smiles, spinning down the hall, some thick, others thin and

tall.

Braided locks, flying with a slightly red tint, others very black, hanging loose and

slack.

Wonderful things among my peeps to see; brought sweet, sweet memories to an

O.G.

Yes, hear it, feel it, and see it too: Brown, Black, Asian and White brothers; pride in being, brightly

shining through.

Here was woman, here was man; God's beautiful colors in America's White, White,

land.

Proud, we saw our children, young women and men; filling that education space, again and again.

Such benign feelings; among the many shades of those walls; the world is yours to take my children,

"Walk tall! Walk tall!"

9th Grade Class: Is just that, about a typical day in a 9th grade classroom of an inner city school in the Bay Area of Northern California. Sometimes questions bring answers we are uncomfortable hearing.

9th Grade Class

In history class we talk about the past, about what happened during our yesterdays: A record of those things that happened; reflected in various ways.

Remember, what happened to you yesterday personalizes your history. "Well last night I got high, fought two scraps; and then, the cops busted my friend and…"

"Did you finish your homework?" "Yeah, teach, but then I had to cuss out my momma before school today."

"The bitch tried to tell me not to talk to her that way; I smacked her, what could I say?"

WA alaikum salam: Following 9-11 we all felt frustrating outrage at such an act, and an incredible sorrow for those who lost their lives, common folk, not soldiers, their families and loved ones. The consequences are far reaching and continue touching our lives in so very many unanticipated ways.

WA alaikum salam

Alone in the schoolyard again today; hijab covered head, down, forward and turned away. What's on her mind, living in this time? Listen to the news, know our blues; repetitiously stated, self created. I child in school, what did she do; born into the same world as me and you?

Religion and culture, does that change things; or, are some Americans less than others; for some, does freedom not ring? What happened 'over there' how does it affect us here? We all have an 'over there' in our pasts somewhere. Does anyone care?

The blood and pain of another land, here, should it touch a child's hand? Do we hurt children for things they haven't done; because of the lands their ancestors are from? In the totality of life, is prejudice and racism a part of the sum?

How may we help; where do we start; how do we change? What does it take to alleviate a brother or sister's pain? Do we pretend it doesn't matter, doesn't pertain; we aren't in it; why make a fuss: Because tomorrow it could be us.

Hello, how you doing, what's up? That's what you say; a few kind words from a kind heart go a long, way. Help others, even when it's not a 'cool' thing to do; as several philosophers put it, Do unto others as you would have them do unto you.

When folk cry, "Help! Help!" Do something; bring the much needed positive change. Fix this thing. Arab, Muslim, do we care? Help is needed; get in there!

Peggy and John: Compadres, an ideal couple with similar pasts; steeped in historical participation in the m usic, songs, and most radical political activity of the 1960's; always and forever good folk.

Peggy and John

Remember those angry white riots the world
watched on TV; in Mississippi, Alabama,
Tennessee, and other states of the Old
Confederacy? Well, among the dogs, the
nightsticks, bricks, guns and bombs were my
friends, Peggy and John. Segregation ended as did
much of the strife, as those two from California
somehow escaped with their life.

Finding each other in Berkeley after many years
had passed, love, marriage and kids came very fast.
Two children and one job, things were kinda tough
until a large inheritance smoothed out the rough.
They moved to the Berkeley Hills; following
flatlands break -ins again and again; reluctant to
file charges against the "... poor Black men."

Their view of the world, though good, I thought
sometimes made no sense; but what the hell; they
live in Berkeley,where the meaning of "sense", or
any other word is of debatable consequence.

So, over the years I made mistake after mistake;
such as giving young Michael a BB Gun for his 9th

birthday. An affront to their non-violent principles; they didn't know what to say.

Far removed from the front lines of politics; we processed our kids through our communities and local schools. Peggy and John: Having thought their neighbors fools for sending their kids to private schools, now faced that very same issue.

Their son Michael was getting jumped several times a week at Berkley High; yet they couldn't understand why he wanted to change schools. They argued that without the public school experience; they could only see a "Whitebread" kind of man which Michael would turn out to be?

 Dragging myself from the floor laughing; I reminded them of how they were treated by white racists in the South during the 60's: Also that racism is a human condition that comes in colors too: Suggesting that maybe they should forget their politics, and send Michael to a school where he is safe, as any parent would do.

Where you Coming From: Is an expression still common; especially in 'OG' conversation. "I don't know where you coming from, sista/brotha." A question once referring to a lack of understanding of what was meant or said has become a question of domicile and/or affiliation with sometimes deadly consequences.

Where you Coming From

To question meaning, to clarify or understand what was said or meant; at one time was to know where a person was 'coming from.'

Today is much the same, as the question, sometimes in different words, remain. Curious folk still want to know which way you go: Though today's answer may be more complicated and weighty than before.

"What up?" The response is much easier than most, just say 'nada' and coast. But, what Color or what you claim, introduces a more serious game: C or B; Blood or Crip; Red or Blue; Norte or

Sur? What do you say? Which do you choose? No choice or wrong choice you lose. When asked, where you coming from; it may help to note the appearance and dress of the asker before you respond.

Your simple answer may carry more weight than one could reasonably anticipate. Check for visible tattoos on the hands, arms and face: Teardrops and dots; the number of each and their location or place. Check the pant legs too, is one rolled up, is it left or right: A Crip or Blood defining sight.

So if by chance you find yourself in an inner city or in areas you rarely if ever go, this may be important information one should know. Remember, Where you coming from, that once neutral positive statement, a common question to ask or say, requires observation of surroundings and caution; before such an utterance today.

VI

"Hi Pop": I like many folk, have been scribbling and making various notes since childhood. But this is by far the hardest thing I have ever written. Here, is the printable civilized version of some of the feelings of the time. The anger, I have yet to find a place for.

"Hi Pop"

I should have known when you kept saying, "No, no." But I kept asking you to run with me like all those times before. Now, you just made excuses, with so many reasons not to go. I should have known when we ran together that one last time; when my slow pace was too fast, you couldn't keep up; falling further and further behind.

On that day, you almost fell, though you'd been running rings around, me since you was under twelve. I should have known when we saw that doctor; the look on his face made me afraid, because his attitudinal vagueness left so much unsaid.

I should have known the precision, since you were a mere toddler; of that recurring vision. A vision showing you as a young adult, on your back, lying so, so still; the feeling in my chest said death, but it made no sense, it couldn't be real.

I should have known that such joy, couldn't last a lifetime beyond a little boy. Love can't change things or make them right; can't push away the darkness and bring back the light. I should have known, when the silence grew; gone were the bonds of humor and athletics, we once knew. I should have known when you spoke of my "...secret life," that you too might suffer, a similar strife.

 I should have known when you walked out the front door for the very last time; nothing noteworthy, or different to see, baby boy walking away with a shoulder slouch, like me. But the vision remained the one I didn't want to see. A vision like others I'd seen, realistically still, nothing like a dream.

It came every year or so, as my son grew; first when he was one, and again when he was two. Again at age four, at five and six; a commonplace unwanted vision that I couldn't fix. The vision of you as a young adult lying so still became reality, needless to say, the pain a constant reminder every single day. The turn of a corner, during my habitual routine, the tears start flowing, an unfettered stream.

Neemie, my son; no longer with us, the repetitive refrain; here for just a minute repeating in my brain: I saw and loved him for the briefest, briefest time; gone to walk with God, he was never really mine. Gotta get out of this hallway, into my room; where tears flow freely, in the singularity of gloom.

Dad misses and needs you son, every second, every day. How I wish there was some method or practical means; to remove this barrier of time, go back and hear you, just once more say;

"Hi Pop."

A Brief Sample Of The unrehearsed jotte d Pain from, "Hi Pop": God took my son and left me with words, words, words, words, words! Those words from the cop who told me first; were followed by words from me in response. Then came my words in response to the cop words to his mother; words from the Los Angeles Coroner's office, words from his brother, words from friends, neighbors, strangers, kids, teachers. Words! Words! Words! I am still spouting useless words that don't fill the void. Words that won't fill the hole in my life! Words, words, words, words, words, words; no matter how many words; not enough! Not enough words! Not enough words!

"Like Your Poetry": There are many endings; we may sometimes think that one was more painful than the other, in retrospect.

"Like Your Poetry"

"Like your poetry," she said. Honey, if you only knew; the source of my expression, should be familiar to you. My poetry is life; pages of my pain: words are bullets; ripping, tearing, and twisting; explosively quiet refrain. My poetry; is it not common, do you not recognize a line, each a gift from you to me; passed over time.

You sit there and make such a statement, bold as can be, oblivious to your presence; writing the words, for all but you to see. "Like your Poetry," you say, a staring beauty, facing her empty closet, ready to move away from me. Careless sista, if you only knew, when you walk out that door, the poetry goes too.

"Like your poetry," you say, tightening straps on your backpack; preparing to go away; California to New York, with the coming day. So many loose pages, you never read, but on this day; you managed to see just one, lying on the bed.

You, are the words I squeeze and dribble onto the page; the essence of all the thoughts, tastes, smells and colors I see; that makes what you call, my "...poetry."

2005

God Help Us: Is part one of four stories; taken from pictures of the war of the time; showing hurt, pain, and the specific randomness of its recipients: Horror stories.

God Help Us

What is the face of death: What is this pain I see? Is it not applicable to an Iraqi? Is it less because it is not us, not I to die? Lowered head, wet eyes, properly you stand; holding it all inside, like a real man. What if you had fallen in the street; yelled as loudly as you could; horror on your face; crawling in the dirt; scraped nails into the wood?

If you tore your pants at the knee; squeezed horrendous hurt in your bloody hand; would that make you less a man? Is this pain I see; less because you are Iraqi; less because it is not I, but the other guy? I see you brother, though only through a photographer's eye, and to say I share your pain; would surely be a lie.

I do feel the sadness, and an overwhelming sorrow; my daily prayer is to rid this earth, of such pain and horror. Knowing the words I pour onto others won't change a thing; but provide relief for me, from the terrible things we see.

They also guide my prayers through the horrors we've come to know, relying on God for a more benign way he'll show.

Friendship: The picture showed 12 US Marines; eight of them on their knees in full combat gear with arms hugging shoulders; while three others stood, heads down sharing tears and sadness. The remains of the 12th Marine on the gurney, legs poking from the encircling praying friends; feet twisted in an unnatural position; compatible with death. The surprise and confusion on the youthful faces of his 'comrades,' shows that even in a war zone, they are new to the experience; death and dying.

Friendship

Dear God bestow mercy on those young men
today; before their friend; what does one say?
Nothing he'd hear: The remains of what he was so
limp, so near. All are staring at the cold, cold
ground; warm tears and prayers quietly falling
down.

Twenty two eyes closed, shading light; praying so
hard, knowing this isn't right. "One minute he was
with us, 'Semper Fi', we were one, then in the blink
of an eye; he's all alone."Alone, no matter how
close they crowd around; an empty shell disguised
as their friend on that cold "S" ground.

He's gone, where souls go, but still they can't
believe; just beginners are they; learning that thing
called grieve. Death, he's dead, he died, muerte;
he's gone; now who'll bring the news, to his family
back home? Gone are the days when news was
slow; a passing glance at CNN, they'll know.

Yes, all are somebody's children, fathers, husbands,
sons, and brothers; who'll be missed by family,

friends, and others. "He was a good boy, loved his country too; hand on heart; he stood when the flag passed; red, white and blue."Patriot, is that the word we use, is that what we say, to grieving family and friends, on this death day?

Only God could turn it around, for the weeping comrades; those twelve Marines in Iraq; those twelve children on the

ground.

Just Iraqis: This from another picture of war with an explanation below reading: "Family Members: mourn a father, his teenage son and a male relative shot and killed by Marines on Wednesday night after they were driving and *allegedly* did not stop while passing U.S. Marines. The family (Mom about 30 with 3 kids all under 12) found out about the deaths when the bloody car was towed home."

Just Iraqis

Hand covered crying eyes; what does he see, the fatherless child's blame, for you and for me. Contorted, squinting, with the agony of grief; tearless stained faced; crying to Allah for relief. The day's present sorrow as it slowly fades, becomes a cancerous hatred with violence homemade; suicide bombers and al-kaeda Kool-Aid.

The young girl's open mouthed scream; is photographically clear, photogenically clean. She stands far, far, from her brother, though very, very near; sounds in the pictured silence, only they can hear. What will she bring, to her short future to come; a mini-skirted model; wearing a roadside bomb?

Baby girl looking at brother, what does she see? Can he feel her emotion and caring for family? Hijab shrouded, eyes closed crying mom; face of excruciating pain; a bleak unthinkable future, all that remains.

Only Iraqis: Is the final of the four writings about the war of the time. It begins with the quote below, credited to our then President of the United States, Bush 2, giving reasons for entering Iraq, overthrowing their government and killing their President as well as thousands of other Iraqis and Americans.

"...Weapons of mass destruction and enough chemicals to destroy a major city; they're only Iraqis, not deserving of our compassion, care or pity."

Only Iraqis

The other day I was listening to some words
floating around, about the war in Iraq; waged in
the air and on the ground. The war words followed
by a picture; flashed a future of dismay; reflected
in the present pain, in the picture I saw that day.
What made this happen; what caused this thing,
words that became weapons of mass destruction?

This crying mother is not Saddam Hussein! Does
death have a color, ethnicity on its face; reserving
its visits for one race?

Four standing broken beyond anguish, from an
accidental twist; somebody should help them; but
only God can fix this. Inadvertent destruction;
intentional/unintentional pain; delivery is
immaterial; it feels the same. We know of
accidents, of death too, the relentless hunter,
nothing remains.

See the grief, look into her eyes; put yourself in her
place, feel the tears she cries; endure the suffering;
as your loved one dies. Feel what she feels for the

living that must go on; help her raise those children; dear God; in the midst of a war zone, she can't do it alone.

Protect them from the bad that lurks while they play, waiting for the right moment to snatch them away. God help them in every way; not in this lifetime, or after, will they forget today.

I am, oh so sorry, dear lady, for this horror, this day; brought to you from my homeland, the U.S. A.

What Did I Say: Slightly changes our tune, although the conversation remains about endings. We remember the background music that accentuates our lives; tunes taking us from beginning to end as they highlight and define key moments of the unique drama. What of the tune makers?

What Did I Say

As I listen to the men and songs I claim as mine,
grateful to God for the beauty of their

rhyme.

The beauty of the sounds, transcendent of time,
brings joy to the soul and peace to

mind.

Those singers of songs, special of men, takes you
places you are going and places you've

been;

adding a timeliness to a life that bespeaks an

end.

Can beauty die; does a certain sound pass too?
Does that body tingling feeling ever leave me and
you?

Remember that day we met, I a much younger
man, overflowing admiration; proud to shake your
hand.

Knowing that time would come, I blacked out the day, when I'd no longer hear, the sweet sound of Brother Ray.

What did U say? I miss you today, 'always and forever' Brother Ray, Brother Ray.

Here, alone you left us on an American Beautiful Day, knowing the transition, shouldn't be any other way.

A prayer for only; love, harmony and godliness, in the wake of Brother

Ray.

(In memory of Brother Ray Charles, 2004)

Conversations End: Too is about endings and the sadness that it often brings. I don't remember if I left or she left. I suspect I did as I try to put a face to the writing. I've narrowed it down to two people. I'm not with either one today, so 'Conversations End' could possibly have applied to either, though I think, a cold thought, that I may have left one of the two for the other.

Conversations End

Days tinged with sadness, brushed by

tragedy;

paints a picture of sorrow, passed to you from

me.

Color the depths of oneness, with strokes wide and

bold.

Add the lurking shadows; tall, quiet, alone and

cold.

Watch Meeting: Was a common part of the Southern Black Community. Often they lasted 24 hours or more. Held in churches or homes, gratefully; I was always on the outer fringes of the event. But I did participate in one.

Watch Meeting

I was Poppa's favorite, or so the brothers and sister told me as adults. Thinking back and listening to their explanations of how they knew; I think that that may have been true.

Molasses slow morning; heavy hints of dread; Poppa, in my 16 years, always the first out of bed. Not today. Poppa always found excuses to encourage me in school; bragging to the neighbors: "That Donnie, he ain't nobody's fool!"

Later, I walked into the living room where Poppa now sat with Mama Tang and Miss. Mildred; a neighbor from across the street. This was odd, because Poppa rarely sat with others; especially outsiders.

Focused concentration; mentally and physically trying to see; I looked hard at Poppa, saying nothing; unblinking eyes looked back at me. A sound in her voice with a hint of dread: "Poppa is a little sick, we're going to see the doctor;" Tang said.

In my 16 years; Poppa had never been sick. He'd never seen the doctor. This couldn't be; I looked again at Poppa; now lowering his eyes; showing, what I didn't want to see. Eyes about the room as my intensity grew; three bowed heads; then I knew.

They went to the doctor, returned in a bit, nothing to discuss: And began the watchful, waiting, sitting; poignant, silent; misery: the serenity of unstoppable ends; as it enveloped us.

Slowly with expression, "I'm going to bed." only I looked at him, witnessing the gravity, the lonely, simplicity, of what Poppa said.

More hours of sitting, late into the night; watching and waiting for the inevitable, unmentionable; unwelcome sight. Tang finally said, "Donnie, go check on Poppa." We all knew before I stood; what I was going to see; reluctantly, moving toward Poppa's door; fear walked with me.

Cold room, pictures on the walls, pipe on its stand; everything in its place; Poppa; lying stiff toed, on his back; open mouth, fright filled eyes of pain and death, on his ashen face.

Tock: is about time and the ancient sound by which it was once measured; nowadays rarely if ever heard; tick tock. Tock is also about forced interactions with unfriendly strangers, and other folk you don't wish to know.

Tock

Time, the thief, who steals your living soul; takes the man you once knew, and leaves a stranger old. He's there when I walk past the mirror; don't recognize who I see; the wrinkled, faded, ancient face; staring back at me.

Can't speak what was spoken yesterday, so out of date; not PC; so pase'! Daily peering with eyes so old, from the depths of memories, untold: You were once the brightest light from that yellow shaded lamp, now shining through the dusty motes of eternity's ramp.

Faded post, brown rusted stand, reflections from the body of an aged Black man: Time, what is this thing; but an inexorably, emotionless, aging intruder; that life surely brings.

Out for a run; as fast as I can, with not enough speed to pass the walking man: Time, much more than the ticking of the clock; the truth of the passing is surely in the tock.

Black Like You: Looks to the history of human ancestry and the homo sapiens group who managed to outlast others and survive to this day.

Black Like You

Then there are those who don't like this color that they see; which means absolutely nothing to me. Should I care that you don't like Black, or about the miniscule mentality reflecting such a lack?

Lack

of knowledge of the source of human kind; this group of earth occupying homo-sapiens; to which we are all aligned.

Knowledge

of the Leakey's and their findings at Oulduvai; the continuity of the species that leads to you and I.

I

am a child of Oulduvai and so are you; add DNA to the story, that the Leakey's already knew.

Knew

the DNA trail starts in the homo-sapien homeland; wherefrom they covered the globe; this dominating woman and man.

Man

like other plants and animals, he did adapt, to the environmental conditions of his new home, on this earthly map.

Map

a trail leading northward to far cooler climes; shaded and protected from the sun's direct rays.

Rays

of direct sunlight, no longer there; hence loss of the cranial shading, ancestral curl of the hair.

Hair

Is just part of the homo-sapien brew, because of location; skin protecting melanin goes too.

To

each remained a remnant shading; light or dark; dependent on the global location, where the ancestor parked.

Sadly, that loss of color, as many know, is directly related to where our ancient relatives decided to

go.

Yes, a particular shade, because of the choices, long dead ancestors made.

So, remember, whatever your present shade may be; your ancestral mother wore dreadlocks; and

was Black like me!

Choices/Chance: After high school and the military; I moved to Los Angeles to live with my older brother while working and attending college. One weekend at a party, I was surprised to see someone I had grown up with. Greeting 'Buck' Pruitt enthusiastically, I shook his hand. Noticing his reserve, his coolness; an awful high school memory we shared came back to me. This story speaks to that memory.

Choices/Chance

We didn't have to do it, the way it all came down,
but we thought our choices limited in that small
town. As high school seniors; the habitual threats
from sophomores, we all laughed off. But when we
bigger folk weren't around, they'd find the smallest
of us alone, and beat him down.

When Charles got jumped a second time, they
laughed and bragged about what they'd done, we
looked around our various households, for the
family gun. The Friday Sock-Hop in the gym was the
time the 10th grade boys picked, promising any
senior showing up; would get his ass kicked.

Although outnumbered five to one, we were
seniors; sophomores wouldn't make us run. I don't
remember who suggested it, or how it came about;
the working plan that changed things and turned
the fight into a rout. Where did it begin, how did it
come to be: Brothers fighting Brothers; made no
sense to me.

Sophomore girls dating senior boys seemed such a
childish thing, but judgment lies in the

repercussions that an act may bring. Seniors, just months before graduation: Certain we had it 'made'; much more than a boy, just in the 10th grade.

So, girls the reason for the fuss, now down that dark, concrete gray sidewalk; forty angry tenth graders, stood cussing in front of us. The comments grew louder, from the group we could see; but we were prepared as we'd planned to be.

Charles with a 45, barrel cold on his right thigh; alongside Scott; shotgun under his coat; stock poking very high: Sanders had a 38 and so did I. In the quiet of the night and the cold, cold air, Charles threw open his coat, with a theatrical flair.

We others did the same; weapons show and tell; offering personal, invitations to hell. Charles at the front of the line, the gym very near, as I covered the rear, watching an uninvited spectator join us, named fear.

The yell was loud; in the silence, a shout: "Donell look out!" From the corner of my eye, as I spun around; I saw a baseball bat in Buck's hands, near my head; coming down. Grabbing the bat with my left hand, and the 38 with the other; I pressed it to Buck's ear, as he fell to the ground.

Didn't hear the click, as I pulled the trigger, Buck's cry: "Lord don't let him kill me!", or Charles' sarcastic snigger. "Fucking gun!"! I said at the misfire, as buck lay squirming, still down. Suddenly, like a scene from a movie, everything slowed; scanning the crowd, looks of horror, a face- shot tableau, profound.

Pulling the trigger again; this time I heard the click, louder than the expected explosion; in a silence thick. The action had moved from the front to the back; eyes of horror on Buck with a gun to his head; lying flat, undead.

There, in a place I'd never been; instead of observing outside violence; I was on the inside looking in. Someone yelled:"Hal's coming!" Hal was our one local cop. Quickly disappearing into places to hide; sophomores and seniors, ran side by side.

Wondering whether it worked, Charles and I tested the weapon in the fields behind our house the following day: Two heated explosions; rocked my hand; burning any doubts about the 38 away.

Am I so different from the man locked down; or sitting on death row? In this vein, I suspect we are all much the same, so my answer must be no.

Where is that contrived difference, where is the line? Is demarcation so sublime? We just acted, didn't stop to think, consider, ponder at all; is it merely by chance, where the chips may fall?

VII

Ain't that **the truth.':** Refers to a societal rarity; those who dare question. To dare question authority is to be "argumentative": Nowadays a killing offense.

"Ain't That The Truth!"

Some see it daily, but dare not speak out. Yes, they're aware, they know; grew up during a different time, in this same country; but then of a different mind. Now aged and gray, who'd listen to anything they have say?

A system fed by state run media, perpetuating myths, day after day. Just give them money, and they say what the government wants them to say. Media control is the key, to handling a spoon fed citizenry.

They've been trained to believe what they're allowed to see: What they watch and what they're told is their reality. The truth all know, because they saw or heard it on a TV show. News, sports, weather, movies, music, theatre, dance and literature; are all pushing the same themes; after the state tells them what it all means. Daily, as the noose tightens (unnoticed by most), many are reluctant to say, things that may be contrary to the state way.

Truth seekers just listen to the news, and believe what they say, on all channels; again and again, 24 hours a day. Using the same "Talking Points", they are called in this modern time, although that other word, indoctrination, also comes to mind.

Not very long ago folk knew; saying the same thing over and over again, didn't make it true! For such absurdities, one was called a fool; but nowadays, with talking heads like 'say it again' Wolf Blitzer, repetition is the rule.

When Asians Had No Titty: Is about the foods that are at the forefront of American diplomacy and the exciting changes they have wrought on the world stage.

When Asians Had No Titty

Hera are a few things with certainty, we used to know; though still pretty, there was a time when Asians had no titty: Unless of course they were from the South, which was a different call; because the lighter North Asians didn't consider South Asians, Asian at all. They being dark you see, brought into question their right to be, Asian.

Truly a time of interesting themes, when only Black folk knew how to dance and sing; they could run fast, and jump high too; but things like thinking, they just couldn't do. Others could dance a little bit and look the cutey, but only Black chicks could shake that booty.

Beauty does not stand alone, always contested, since before the days of stone: Waiting in the wings was that other; with additional attributes to make them pretty. Shadings of color, or lack thereof, may be positives too; as well as the larger titty.

However, the titty may encompass a worldly scene involving government, trade finance, agriculture and massive intended and unintended cultural exchange. One would think that government would take the lead; not so, Colonel Sanders was one of the first to go; beyond walls and borders, to places where fried chickens folks didn't know.

Asia, with Africa, and Latin America, all jumped into the ring; with body shaping changes that certain foods bring. Adding McDonalds to the world mix was an additional guarantee for the body we'd see. Hence the creation of a fat based new world pretty; enhanced rumps for all and a fine, fine titty.

Tree Climbing: Do you remember the last time you ran as fast as you could, did a handstand, jumped as high as possible; skipped a rock; or cannonballed from the high dive? When did you last climb a tree? Why did you stop doing those things?

Tree Climbing

Saw the perfect tree today; got that old urge to climb, that never goes away. Low sloping limbs, curving gently upward from the ground with tactically placed outgrowing branches; perfect for hands. I could be up from the street, nesting among the low greenery in less than two feet.

Is it wrongful to have such thoughts walking past that gentle giant each day: Knowing that if I tried to climb her or any of her kind, I'd immediately be locked away? I've climbed trees, jumped from hills; splashed puddles and ran for no reason other than the joy I felt. Possessed of the same mind and body from then, why can't I do those things again?

"Fool you're old!" My wife said once more, as if I didn't know. "It doesn't matter what you feel now or what you felt then," **Continuing in a lecturing tone:** There are certain courtesies and rules for living in society that dictate actions for certain ages; necessary to maintain stability."

"What of my stability?" I asked." I'm a 'baby boomer' there are more of us than them!" **Undaunted she continued:** "Old people climbing trees you see, would be a threat to the younger, non-'climbing members of society Your action would get in the way of their turn to climb trees; It's their tree, their **day**!"Yes it's true, **she said with**

a smile, "If you climb, they will certainly ask me to sign, to have you put away."

To be acceptable for a positive blend, one must act a certain way; do old people things to comfortably fit in. Bingo and cruises are good, and scrabble too: So is a cane, a walker or a noticeable limp. Doesn't hurt to forget the month or day; and act befuddled now and then. All adds to ones value and lessens the chance, that you'll be put away.

No, age is not a crime; but, there are penalties for living a long time.

Ella's Soul Food Café: Speaks to the foods of those southern Blacks; many whose families came to California following the World Wars in the first and second Great Migrations'. Ella's is also a positive response for those doing the hard work of living in previously all-white suburbia.

Ella's Soul Food Café

Felt good to be back in Oakland; briefly home a while ago; to sniff the welcoming smells as I walked in the door. But Oakland is home, no matter where you from; a fine reception for people of color all and one.

Over the years, not much ahs changed, a bit older, but familiar faces remain. The same family cooking and waiting today; some were mere toddlers when I first came this way.

Grits and eggs in the morning; collard greens, cornbread and gumbo for the afternoon: And always, always; the sweet smell of chitlins permeates the room.

I dare not question Ella's wisdom year after year, like the other Black refugees from suburbia; Ella knows why we are here. The 1960's and 70's in the Bay Area were especially fine; back then, not just at Ella's. Black folk were still Black most of the time.

Like me many of those same Blacks still come in; with their children and sometimes even their children's children;who are African-American women and men.

Listening to the same juke box tunes as I've done on my returns over the years I patiently wait to hear welcoming me in , once again: From somewhere in the kitchen, Ella's shout: "I know brother Williams, those white folks wear you out!"

Public Transit USA: Traveling over the years I've spent a lot of time in stations and Airports. Also on, trains, planes buses and taxis. After a few years you see the same public transit works, legal and illegal. All are generally tolerated by the police and transit authorities as just another part of the transit system.

Public Transit USA

See them on trains, buses and public transit boarding platforms day after day. They too are going to work, but in a different way. Well built, muscular Black and Asian men; harvesting fear from inherent racism without and within. Within their small minds all whites and certain Asians are weak, racist and rich; easy prey without a hitch. Prey indoctrinated with the racist fear of the 'big mean Black man' perpetuated by the media, police and Hollywood year after year.

Standing close the demand is made: "Give me a dollar!" Dare the smaller white man say no: For just a dollar the scary colored will step aside so he can go? Working their sections of the trains, buses and stations day after day: Harassing and robbing white riders and making a living that way. Black riders too, pretend they don't see while other whites and light skinned Asians say: "Thank God it's not me."

Stereotypes, racism and fear bring silence to those who see this day after day; week after and dare not speak. Overheard on one BART train: "Those poor Blacks need the money: There are no jobs for those Black men honey." Even if a believer in such simplistic racist trash; does that give one the right to take another's cash? Fools of any color can see a robbery. Although Justice may peek sometimes; to maintain a' civil society' we must still pretend that she is blind.

Some still think it wrong when the weak are taken advantage of by the strong. They may even believe that right has no color, much the same as wrong. But can we even say it? Can we say what we see, even if it's not PC? Young Black men are preying on public transit riders in major cities across the country. There I said it! Woe is me? Daily, that's what they do and it affects all colors, because we all are Americans too: And robbery is not what we condone or do.

Closed eyes and ears are the easy way out, which perpetuates the racism and hooliganism that we're talking about. For some the solution is simple, bring in more cop, But bringing in their additional racism, simple it is not. They'd love to come in with an unrestrained hand: Indiscriminately, joyfully, breaking all Black and Brown heads again and again.

The local police and the transit workers know who the local thugs are, but don't care; on public transit, no high profile citizens are there. So, what remains, must it stay the same? Dare we speak up and let the thugs know, or buy into the stereotypes and let them go? "They can't help it, Blacks are thieves!" as we all know.

Respite: There is a way to avoid the transit hustlers and other travel thugs. Retirement may take one to new ways and places to travel: Maybe?

Respite

Must pause and think here; research and see, the options offered me..

Retire today? Get out while I can? Is it time to go? Do Conditions portend?

If I go now, the slate is still clean. I haven't reacted to the reality and

mean.

I know, look for the good in every soul, pass on the detriment to the next

Hole.

With eyes open wide, intake the scene: Living by fate obscures the scene.

Little monies, stashed here and there: Is retirement the end: Is it the

where?

Stop the work, less money to see; does this mean living uncomfortably?

If you gonna take out you gotta put in: That's how it's always been.No work, no pay! No toil no reward! You can't win if you don't play! A penny saved is a penny earned: Isn't that what we all learned?

The Beginning (Cuba Trip) Day 1 July 14 2010.

Bart Screams: Was written soon after an unarmed Black man was shot and killed by a policeman while being held face down on a BART Station passenger loading platform by other policemen. I just happened to be riding BART soon thereafter and noticed the tension and some major differences between BAY Area Rapid Transit (BART) and the New York City Subway System.

BART Screams

While the New York City Subway System silently rocks and flows, BART scrunches and screams, though tensions on both clearly show. The postures of the people, quickness of the glancing stare on BART: though no subway stares; the firm barriers between the seats are noticeable, though physically not there. Thankful survivors relish the end of the ride, happier places to go among people they

know.

Subway gently rocking with a quiet roar; BART screams loudly, for all to ignore. Words short and harsh from the ticket monitor, coming real fast; brother to brother for a simple question asked. All aboard, more of the same, Asian White glances: United hatred on the moving

train.

A moment's pause; beginning to see, this isn't about me, a reaction to the verdict; as the Black passenger killing cop goes free. Yep, manslaughter, time served, free he could very well be. Me: Just a Black outsider passing through, who also feels the fuss: White hot hostility, directed at all of us?

Is the hostility a reflection of the guilt felt for the killing of an unarmed passenger or does it reflect the joy of killing a Black Man? Looking closely at the eyes I tried to see whether they'd do the same to me. The hate in the eyes of the BART police is not disguised, , overflowing, it's there too. When they see Black men hate is what cops

do.

Standing on the platform, unarmed, I gave it right back; knowing his cop habits, I don't even have to try, to match the hatred I see in his eye. Strange, it may seem to some, the imputation to all for the color of

one.

DW 7-2010

Dreamer: Is a brief story about one of many recurring dreams I have about my kids and my family during that time when they still played with their parents.

Dreamer

Kids and I down the hill, playing we

three.

Large shady, low limbed tree; fire pits, open green yard

was beautiful to see.

Gotta get back up the hill and lock the open house.

The wife

should be here too: I was thinking hard about that;

the family,

all together; and that's where I'm at.

The jokes

on me it seems, as I awaken to a past, inexplicably

painful,

incomprehensibly unforeseen.

A

Horrible nightmare of a lonely man, masked in the joy of a family dream.

Gas Stop In Texas: The three of us had known each other since elementary school back in Arkansas where we now decided to visit. Like many young Black folk living in Los Angeles at the time we were armed 24/7; especially when traveling in the South. Down there, all necessary stops and interactions were tense.

Gas Stop In Texas

The California to Arkansas trip, we took year after year; to visit

family

and friends in that place of violence, hatred and

fear.

The homeland, the South, we well knew; the birthplace, and until age 18, where we lived and

grew

From California, to Arizona. New Mexico and then; entering Texas, we began to feel the change; back in the South

again.

Started in Los Angeles with the sunrise, until late into the night; tank

on empty and a Texas gas stop is in sight

We are a bit more watchful here: California plates, a special thing to see, as is our color in the Old

Confedracy

Lucky seven in a line of ten travelers waiting to pay; one clerk at the counter; the late night shift, of her long

day.

Wearing a white t-shirt with cigarette pack in the rolled up sleeve, on arms thick as thighs; crew cut head, with blond stubble on his chin; I watched him walk

in.

.Snatching a bag of pork skins from the rack and a beer from the cooler, he moved to the line and joined

us.

The red pimples on the back of his squat neck were easy to see; because he decided to step into the line in front of

me

With the wide pimply neck, dominating my eyes, I reached for the right rear pocket of my

Levi's..

The young clerk; much wiser than I, and the young racist fool about to

die;

stepped away from the line, moved to a neutral spot at the counter and said to me: "Sir may I help

you?"

Walking toward the clerk now standing to the side of the line at the counter, past 'quello rojo' and paying my bill; as I repocketed my

32.

Poppa: Here a brief memory of my grandfather who we called 'Poppa". Poppa was easily the wisest man I have ever known: He was also very old.

Poppa

I remember Poppa's shaking hands spilling his morning coffee; indiscreet, big eyed; we

watched.

I remember Poppa's hair; the wood stove in the kitchen; on a cold winter day, I cut around the ball spot; falling lumps of gray.

Green papered walls, metal bed, rocking chair, a big trunk in the closet were all in Poppa's room with two shotguns, in the corner against the

wall.

I remember the stories Poppa would tell of life down in the quarters, of America's unfinished

hell.

"No Poppa doesn't know his birthday": Mama Tang said to me. "Well, he was a slave, you

see."

No I didn't see. If Poppa was a slave, how could he be there with

me?

I remember Poppa in Mr. Fish's Store; making an
"X" where it said signature

below.

I remember Poppa on the sidewalk downtown;
hatred in the white man's

eyes;

looking hard at Poppa, because he would not step

aside.

A walk downtown, much for a child to see; Poppa
and

me.

Unsolicited Conversations: I am surprised to discover that there are people who will approach and start a conversation with complete strangers: ME.

Unsolicited Conversations

I don't care that you "…don't see color; that your best friend is Black; your favorite music is rap and R& B. You don't see color, do you also tell such a story to white people you hardly know? If you only see colors lack; why must your best friend be defined as

Black?

A world without color: A scary thought: It would have no clouds, skies, sunrises, sunsets, rainbows, oceans, green fields or any of the other varieties of life's tinge; defining the spaces we live

in.

A maddening rush to say it isn't so, may help define the racists we used to know. Today they don't exist; a thing of the distant past; especially among those in homogenous situations. It's easy to love the night, when everything is white.

I do see color in all of us and all things, and like what I see: In your reality, I can't be, you don't see

color; hence, you don't see me.

Made in the USA
San Bernardino, CA
05 October 2013